Soundless

Silence

A Sherlock Holmes Novel

M. KATHERINE CLARK

Cover Design by Kate Roth (www.katerothwrites.com) and Ashton Clark

Editing by Ashton Clark

Based on the beloved characters created by Sir Arthur Conan Doyle. It is written in the language of the time with certain racial slurs that were used. The author does not condone nor agree with such language or usage. The Author recognizes the use of historical facts and previously published worked, she takes no ownership of said items.

ISBN-13: 978-0-9909915-0-2

Other Works by M. Katherine Clark

The Greene and Shields Files:
    Blood is Thicker Than Water
    Once Upon a Midnight Dreary
    Old Sins Cast Long Shadows
    Tales from the Heart, Novelettes
Soundless Silence a Sherlock Holmes Novel
The Rest is Silence, an Edmond Holmes Novel – Coming Soon
Love Among the Shamrocks Collection:
    Under the Irish Sky
    Across the Irish Sea
    On the River Shannon
    The Land Across the Sea, an Emmet O'Quinn Short
Love Among the Shamrocks Collection, The Next Generation:
    In Dublin Fair City
    Song of Heart's Desire
    Chasing After Moonbeams – Coming Soon
The Wolf's Bane Saga:
    Wolf's Bane
    Lonely Moon
    Midnight Sky
    Star Crossed
    Moon Rise
    Moon Song, a Companion
Silent Whispers, a Scottish Ghost Story
Dragon Fire
    Heart of Fire
    Will of Fire – Coming Soon

Dedicated to my mother whose love of Sherlock Holmes
inspired this story.
With thanks to Sir Arthur Conan Doyle for his genius in creating a
character beloved across time!

"The game's afoot:
Follow your spirit, and upon this charge
Cry 'God for Harry, England, and Saint George!'" – Henry V,
William Shakespeare

"The keen edge of the sword was honed on the rough stone; the sweet scent of the plum blossom was born in the midst of winter's icy grip..." - *Anonymous Chinese Poem, date unknown*

Chapter One

"Of Mrs. Hilton Cubitt, I only know that I have heard she recovered entirely and that she still remains a widow, devoting her whole life to the care of the poor and to the administration of her husband's estate."

"What's that you say, Watson?" Sherlock Holmes asked as he reclined on the chaise lounge, his eyes closed.

"Just finished writing up the Cubitt case," Watson admitted.

"Oh," Holmes answered disinterested, "and what sordid title did you come up with for this one?"

"Sordid?" Watson answered, then continued with a sigh. "I've called it the *Adventure of the Dancing Men.*"

"The Dancing Men?" Holmes exclaimed incredulously.

"Why, what's wrong with it?" Watson asked.

"Watson, I've allowed you to write up my little

exercises in criminal detection, but I absolutely draw the line at allowing you to name them silly little names like the *Dancing Men.*"

Holmes turned over in a huff. After a moment, Watson pushed away from his desk.

"What would you like me to name it, then?"

"How should I know? God only knows how you've romanticized it," Holmes replied, then dropped his voice to a languid tone. "It was a thoroughly disinteresting case, if I recall." Standing, he went to the mantelpiece and took out one of his cigarettes.

"You didn't think so at the time," Watson said.

"Still, one or two minor interesting points," Holmes struck a match and lit the tobacco. "But you take my simple exercises and make them something more. Honestly, Watson, I don't know how you live with yourself. You've disillusioned ninety-nine percent of London."

"What would you have me do then?" Watson questioned. "The public wants to know these things."

"I don't know, they seemed to handle it perfectly well when I was dead," Holmes spat, staring into the fire. He raised the cigarette to his lips and took a long draw. When Watson did not speak for a moment, Holmes turned to look at him. "What's the matter with you?"

"Confound it, Holmes, don't you realize what you put me through? What Mrs. Hudson went through? We thought we lost you! Three years. Three years, Holmes! And what did you do? Just walk away from everything and everyone who loves you! Dear god man, are you so heartless you really think I cared so little?"

Holmes stared into the fire processing Watson's rebuke. The doctor sat back in his chair letting the silence grow between them. It was a long time before he heard Holmes speak.

"You forget, it was for your safety and that of Mrs. Hudson, I stayed away," he said in a low voice.

Not wanting a confrontation for old sins, Watson changed the subject quickly.

"Holmes, you are over-worked and tired." Seeing the

two tickets sticking out of a compartment in his desk, he continued. "You need a distraction. It just so happens I have two tickets to Pierre Bastion tonight. You're coming with me."

"Who?" Holmes asked brusquely.

"Pierre Bastion, he's the great illusionist and clairvoyant," Watson explained.

"Clairvoyant? Illusionist?" Holmes demanded. "Why on earth would I want to sit for an hour and a half watching someone do cheap tricks and swindle Londoners out of their money?" He then thought a moment. "Why, when I can do that right here in the comfort of my own home? You go, Watson, you two seem to have so much in common."

"You're coming," Watson ordered. ignoring Holmes' last remark. "Eight-thirty."

Holmes went to his room and slammed the door. Mrs. Hudson knocked and walked in.

"Is he in a mood?" She asked softly, bringing in that day's post.

"You know what he's like after a case, Mrs. Hudson," Watson replied. "God help us until he gets another one."

"Well, I've brought the afternoon post, Doctor," she answered. "There's one of them letters he always gets excited about. Maybe that'll put him in better spirits."

"Any idea who sends them?" Watson asked.

"None, Sir," she replied.

"Common paper, no scent, no distinguishing marks, I've always wondered. He gets one every day."

"I know, sir, I've been too worried to ask him about it. He could only get upset."

"Well, if he wants to tell us he will," Watson replied accepting the letters. "Post, Holmes," he called.

Holmes burst out of his room and rushed to him. Snatching the letters, he went through them quickly throwing those he didn't want over his shoulder. Finally, his eyes found the one he received every day. Without speaking, he went back to his room and slammed the door.

Holmes and Watson took their seats. Watson was full of anticipation. Holmes begrudgingly slunk down in the seat and crossed his arms, his chin resting on his chest. Looking down his long, thin nose, he watched the footlights flicker on the stage. Grumbling something, as the curtain went up and the show began, Watson nudged him to make him stop.

Throughout the evening, Holmes leaned over to Watson and commented;

"There were two women, one is still in the box."

"Shh," Watson replied.

Then later;

"That has a fake bottom."

"Holmes, shh."

"Oh, come now," Holmes whispered harshly. "It's painfully obvious how he's doing it."

"Holmes, please. I beg you, shh."

The illusionist looked out to the audience hearing Watson's pleading and Holmes' indifference.

"It appears we have a skeptic in our midst," the illusionist said. "You, Sir," he gestured to Holmes. "You don't believe in the supernatural?"

"There are perfectly logical explanations to everything you've done tonight," Holmes answered.

"Holmes," Watson cautioned.

"No, no... doctor..." deducing Watson's occupation, he went on. "Please it's all right. One does not perform before such a crowd without overcoming a few skeptics. You are a Doctor of Medicine, I see. Retired."

"Why yes, I am. I am Doctor Jo—."

"Please, Sir," Bastion interrupted him. "I do not want any names. It could influence me. No, no, you are a retired army doctor. I would say, Afghanistan. You were wounded in the shoulder. You are brilliantly loyal to this man," his attention turned to Holmes. "Hmm, very interesting. Would you allow me, sir?" Pierre asked Holmes, but he did not wait for a reply. "A proud man, one of great mind, but I see you carry a great secret one you wish no one to know; something that shakes the very foundation of who you are. You have kept it from everyone, save one. Your... brother knows... but not this man.

"I see travel. You travel a great distance to conceal this secret. It has dark beginnings. I see pain, blood, you were shot by someone. That started the secret. You wanted to protect someone. Someone you love. I see an enemy who is very close to you, no, no, wait. Not an enemy, a love. The person you love, you want to protect. This person is very close to your enemy. Four people, four distinct lives, yet you are the one who holds the bond together. They're all around you, influencing you, guiding you… especially one, someone you hold very dear, someone… you strive to be better than who you are because she sees you differently… they're your—."

Holmes stood quickly forcing Pierre to go quiet. Everyone, including Watson, looked up at him surprised. Holmes stared hard at the illusionist for a long moment.

"It is *my* secret to keep," Holmes' voice was barely audible but the force behind it drew a shiver from Watson. Again, there was silence as Holmes walked out of the theater.

Watson gathered his coat and followed Holmes finding him outside.

"Holmes, wait," Watson called rushing to catch up with him.

"I need to be alone, Watson."

"My dear fellow, you're as pale as a ghost. What happened to you in there? What was he talking about? Someone you love, you want to protect? Four people? A secret? Your brother? Tell me."

"So you can write it up in your fiction?" Holmes demanded. Watson's stunned stare haunted him.

"Because I am your friend," Watson stated.

After a few moments, Holmes looked down.

"I'm sorry, Watson, I cannot just yet. I must be alone," Holmes turned away, his head hanging low and his walking stick slung over his shoulder. He disappeared into the fog.

Chapter

Two

Watson woke the next morning at his usual time and headed down the stairs to the study for breakfast. Yawning from the inconsistent sleep he had received from that night, he opened the door expecting to smell Holmes' first tobacco of the morning.

"Morning, Holmes," he called but the study was empty.

Unsure if Holmes had come back the night before, Watson went to the stacks of envelopes from the morning post but did not see anything important.

Sitting down at the breakfast table he saw Mrs. Hudson had laid a small breakfast and soon understood why. A note from Holmes lay on his plate.

Watson—
Gone to the South of France for a time.
Expect a telegram when I'm returning.
SH

Watson sighed. That was just like Holmes. Every time

after a case, he would go to the South of France, it could be in the middle of the night and he would always be gone at least a fortnight. He would never ask Watson to go with him.

The usual questions of *why* and *what for* plagued the doctor, but when there were no answers, he took the napkin, placed it in his collar and began to eat.

"Mr. Mycroft Holmes to see you, your majesty," the herald announced in the thick Scottish brogue indicative of the Scottish Highlands where Balmoral Castle was located.

"Mr. Holmes," Queen Victoria smiled as Mycroft bowed. She walked over from the window and extended her hand to him. He bowed over it and kissed the frail fingers through the sheer black lace. "It is good to see you."

"And you, majesty," he said.

"Please pour yourself something to drink," she offered, seating herself in one of the armchairs.

"Thank you, ma'am," he replied going to the sideboard and taking the decanter of Highland Single Malt.

"I can order some soda if you require; John never did take any," she said.

Mycroft bowed but refused silently. For Victoria to mention her former groom; John Brown was unheard of after his untimely death a few years ago.

"So, tell me," she started, offering the chair opposite her. "How is everything?"

"All in order, ma'am," he replied.

"Good and will Mr. Edmond be assisting you in the future? I did so enjoy meeting your–"

"Forgive me, ma'am," Mycroft interrupted her. "But I must request you not mention him. One does not know who may be listening."

"Oh nonsense," she answered. "I can assure you, we are quite alone here. Tell me, I am much looking forward to seeing him again. Such a fine young man. What age is he now?"

"But twenty-three, majesty," Mycroft answered, his eyes assessing every crevice. Just because no one saw anyone did not mean there was no one there. Balmoral was heavily laden with secret passageways and Laird's Lugs. Mycroft would do anything to keep Edmond safe. "I can assure you, Edmond will be assisting me at the Home Office from now on."

"Oh marvelous! Such an intelligent, soft-spoken man for one so young," she gushed. "Much like his father, I do believe."

Mycroft grunted his disagreement and drank his whisky.

"Oh, my love," Marguerite sighed handing her husband cognac and sitting snuggly next to him in the crook of his arm. Pulling her close to him, he kissed her tenderly. "I know I said I would never ask, my darling," she went on, "but when will the world learn of us and our secret?"

He sighed gently and stroked her arm; his eyes on the dancing flames of the fire in the fireplace. Sitting alone with her, was one of the things he loved the most.

"Soon, my love," he answered. "Soon it will be safe enough, I promise you. Did I not tell you that day all those years ago? One day the world would know who I really am. I am yours."

"I love you, *mon coeur*," she stated.

He set his drink aside, turned to her and cupped her face in his hands making her look at him.

"And I want you to know, Margot," he went on, pulling her closer to him. "I love you no less than the amount of stars in the sky or sand on the beach. You are my life. You are everything to me."

"As you are to me," she answered and kissed him, tasting the bite of cognac on his lips.

"Mr. Holmes?" Lestrade burst into the study and looked around. Watson looked up from the newspaper he was reading. "Ah, Dr. Watson, can you tell me where Mr. Holmes has got to?"

"Come in, Lestrade, come in. Sit down. I'm afraid Holmes is out of the country for a time. Is there anything I can do?" Watson asked.

"No, no thank you, Doctor, I need Mr. Holmes," Lestrade huffed and sat opposite the doctor. Watson got up and poured two glasses of whisky, tossing Lestrade the Persian slipper filled with tobacco. "It's these murders, ya see, doctor," he started and gladly accepted Watson's glass. "It's gotta stop and we at the Yard are completely in the dark."

"Which case is this, Lestrade? I've read nothing about it in the paper," Watson asked sitting down.

"I should hope not," he answered. "We've taken great steps to prevent journalists from gettin' a hold of it."

"Slow down, Lestrade, slow down, tell me from the beginning," Watson said.

"It's these murders," Lestrade began. "Four, so far."

"Ah, a serial killer, hmm?"

"Indeed."

"West End?"

"No doctor, that's just the thing," he said. "All of these murders have been of Oriental men killed just outside prominent MPs homes. The last one was outside Sir Richard Russell's flat not five hours ago."

"Oh really, Sir Richard?" Watson asked. "I'm not familiar with him."

"The son of Lord and Lady Helmsworth," Lestrade explained.

"Dear me, a peer of the realm, eh?" Watson asked. "Well, if I can be of any service I do hope you will call upon me. If I hear from Holmes, I will be sure to tell him."

Watson could not sleep at all that evening. Finally hearing his watch chime the second hour of the new day, he got up and wrapped his housecoat around himself. Heading down the stairs to the study for a book to read, he saw a flickering light from under the door. Finding his reserve revolver in the umbrella stand just outside the door, he gripped the old gun tightly. Slowly turning the doorknob he opened the door as quietly as he could.

Holmes stood, fully dressed in his travel attire, leaning against the mantle, a roaring fire in the fireplace, a glass of whisky near his right hand resting on the mantle, and a half-burned cigarette between his fingers on his left hand. He hadn't reacted to Watson's intrusion.

"Holmes," Watson sighed grateful it was not an intruder. "What the devil? I thought you were going to send me a telegram when you were arriving. How was France?" When Holmes did not answer, he took a deep breath and went to bookshelf. Retrieving a book, he headed to the door.

"Come back, Watson, take a seat."

"I had no wish to disturb you," Watson replied. Holmes did not answer and Watson watched him reach for his glass of whisky, taking a long sip. Watson sat on the chaise lounge but when Holmes did not speak for five minutes, he stifled a yawn, and twisted his back subtly to relieve the kinks.

As if making his mind up on something vitally important, Holmes took a deep breath and let it out quickly. Taking the glass, he downed the whisky in one swift move then, he turned to Watson, offering his usual seat in the armchair before the fire.

"I owe you an apology, Watson," Holmes began. Watson stared at him. "An apology and an explanation," he continued. "We have been friends for a very long time now. This is something I should have told you years ago. This may... no it *will* change how you see me." Holmes looked down in his glass, before he continued, he refilled his glass and one for Watson.

"What is it, Holmes?" Watson leaned forward not liking the look on his best friend's face. "You know you can tell me anything."

"I do hope so," Holmes replied.

Less than a half an hour later, Watson sat stupefied, staring at his friend as he finished his tale. Holmes still leaned forward with his elbows on his knees.

"I trust," Holmes finished, "you can understand why I never told you. It happened long before I met you and at the time, I was not sure if I could trust anyone with my biggest secret. When I got to know you better, it was too late to tell you without you thinking I had betrayed you. So you see, I was in a predicament."

Finally, Watson's first words formed.

"But... Holmes, you have always been vastly and most adamantly against that," he said.

"Yes," Holmes agreed. "It's always been an act, Watson. Please know there are other things... more deadly things surrounding this than I am able to share at this time," Watson looked at him and opened his mouth to speak but Holmes held up a hand. "Please, know when I deem it necessary, I will tell you. I promise that, but not now."

"All these years... I've wondered, asked, tried to understand your abhorrence and now... I just do not believe it."

"Why would I lie about this?" Holmes asked.

"I did not say you did... I just... it is a lot to take in," Watson replied.

"John, I swear to you," Holmes started, one of the few times he had called his friend by his Christian name, "I know how difficult it must be considering what you know of me and what I've told you. But I need you to trust me."

Watson pushed out a breath through puffed cheeks and lips.

"It's hard to believe," he said again.

"Would it help if..." Holmes began then looked down.

"What?"

"If you came with me? To see for yourself?"

"You are serious?"

"Quite," Holmes answered. "I think London can do without us for a fortnight and I know the meeting would be beneficial. If you hurry and pack, there is a boat train leaving in forty-five minutes and a train leaving Paris Station in the morning."

Watson observed his friend, trying to see the joke at his expense but Holmes' eyes reflected absolute truth. But... how could he believe him? Knowing everything he did, or thought he did, about Sherlock Holmes. This was too incredible to be believed. And yet... Watson's mind raced with their previous conversations and especially the night at the Illusionist. It all took form and began to make sense.

Taking a deep breath, Watson nodded. He could accept it. He could even understand it. And it made him smile... Sherlock Holmes was human after all.

"All right, Sherlock," he answered using his friend's Christian name mimicking Holmes' earlier sincerity. "I will go with you."

Holmes let out a deep sigh in relief. "Thank you, Watson," he said.

Chapter Three

It was all exactly as Marguerite remembered it. As she stood on the pier looking out at London shrouded in a nighttime fog, she closed her eyes for a moment to wrap herself in the memories that flooded her. It was only after she felt her husband walk up beside her that she smiled and opened her eyes. His grey eyes keenly watched her as she took in the city around them. Taking her hand in his, he raised it to his lips.

"Welcome home, my love," he whispered.

"Home," she repeated. "You are my home." The love reflected in his eyes lightened her heart.

Looking around them, seeing no one, he leaned down and gave her the kiss she had been waiting for. Their eldest son cleared his throat.

"Forgive me for interrupting," Percy said. "But the good doctor was wondering if you could hail a cab, Father."

Marguerite's husband stopped for a moment just watching his eldest with London surrounding them, it was a dream he had held for so long. But there were two missing.

"Where are Edmond and Rebecca?" he asked after his second born.

"Below," Percy replied.

"Tell Ed his uncle is coming to greet us," he said.

"I will tell him," Percy answered. "I know he will be glad to hear that."

Marguerite looked back at her husband and smoothed a wrinkle on his forehead. He leaned into her touch.

"This may be the only time we will have peace, Margot," he said softly. "The newspapers will be hounding us all."

"We are all prepared, *mon cher*," she replied.

"I worry for Rebecca," he said.

"Our daughter is strong," she answered.

"She takes after her mother," he stroked her chin with the back of his fingers.

Marguerite smiled. Even after twenty-five years of marriage, she still felt like a newlywed around her husband.

"What is the strategy then?" she asked.

"My brother has prepared a statement for the press," he explained. "It will be released tomorrow morning."

"So soon?" she asked.

"It must be this way," he replied. "If we wait..."

"*Oui*," Marguerite agreed. "You are right. Well then, I look forward to reading the article."

She kissed him once more, quickly that time, as they heard their three children come up from the boat.

"The doctor is still below, Father," Edmond, their second born, said. "Did Percy tell me correctly? Is Uncle Mycroft coming to meet us?"

"I am already here, lad," Mycroft's voice drew their attention. They recognized his burly figure lumbering up to them in the dim lights of the dock. Edmond smiled widely at him and went to greet him. Marguerite followed, hugging her brother-in-law tightly.

"It is so wonderful to see you again, Mycroft," she said.

"Ah, Margot, the joy is mutual," he said then his eyes turned to her husband. "All is prepared."

"Good," he answered with a deep breath. "Then let the press descend."

"Holmes!" Watson's voice came from the ship. "Will you help me get this confounded contraption off this bloody boat?"

"Doctor, language," Holmes snapped.

Watson appeared from below and, seeing Marguerite and Rebecca, he took off his hat and bowed. "Forgive me, ladies, please."

"You are very strong, Doctor," Marguerite said. "But that is very heavy."

"You know, Watson," Holmes began. "I do have two rather young and strong sons."

"Aye," Watson replied. "But for the love of..." he cleared his throat. "Why did you have another chemical set over in France anyway?"

"That would be for us, Doctor," Percy replied coming up with his brother Edmond. "Please allow us."

"Well, I am not complaining," Watson said taking Holmes' hand to get out of the boat. "Phew," he sighed and wiped his forehead. "I'm getting far too old for this."

"You age like a fine wine, Doctor," Marguerite said. Watson puffed up at her compliment and Holmes stifled a laugh.

"You are too kind," Watson blubbered.

"Not at all," Marguerite answered. Beside her, Rebecca stifled a yawn and asked their pardon. "I fear we all are tired," Marguerite went on. "Perhaps we could return to Baker Street and wait for you gentlemen there."

"I would be happy to escort you both," Watson stepped forward.

"If you would, Watson," Holmes thanked him. "All set there?" Holmes called to Percy and Edmond.

"Done, Sir!" they called back.

"Excellent," he answered. "We follow in the cab behind you." He kissed Marguerite and Rebecca on the cheek and escorted them to their cab. "Let us go home, lads," he said walking back to his sons and Mycroft. "I'd like to be safely ensconced inside Baker Street before the newspaper boys start crying 'Extra'."

"Extra! Extra! Sherlock Holmes' secret revealed!" One boy yelled outside of 221B Baker Street. "The king of detection has a queen! Read all about Sherlock Holmes' secret family! Extra!"

Holmes stood in Baker Street with a roaring fire listening to the paper being read by a strong, slightly French accented voice.

"'Sherlock Holmes shocked the world yesterday by announcing the arrival of four people no one ever thought existed. The great detective revealed he was by no means a confirmed bachelor when he introduced his wife, two sons and daughter to London Society. This revelation comes after the close of one of the most brutal crime sprees since Jack the Ripper. Not much is known about his secret family except they were living on an estate in the south of France.

"'In a private interview with the family, the great detective revealed he had been married for nearly twenty-six years to Marguerite Holmes nee Moreau. Little is known about her, except she and Mr. Holmes met at her family's estate in Yorkshire many years ago before the detective's world-renowned career and association with Doctor Watson.

"'It is known the detective used an alias while over in France and his family used it as their last name. The name *Maison* is the French word for home. In the private interview, this paper was able meet his family, as it is not just his wife but his children as well. Mrs. Holmes is one of the loveliest women on earth.' Quiet so, mama," Edmond complimented quickly and continued reading.

"'Her quiet demeanor and attentive behavior had a way of putting everyone at ease. She is quoted to say she is very happy to finally be back in London and is thrilled to be with her husband after all these years of taking time when he could get away. "He is a wonderful man and I knew when I married him, he would be an even better father and he has never proven me wrong." She stated.

"'Holmes and his wife have three children; Charles,

Edmond, and Rebecca. His devilishly handsome eldest son; Charles Percival Holmes will soon have the hearts of all this seasons' debutants in his hands. He is a fashionable twenty-four-year-old and has an interest in politics. His equally handsome, though less fashionable younger brother, Edmond Weston Julian Holmes, twenty-three, is said to be a virtuoso on the violin, like his father. The youngest of the three is Rebecca Jacqueline Holmes who, the detective and his wife have confirmed, will be presented to society this season. She is said to be one of the loveliest debutants of the season at just seventeen years.' *Bien-sûr*," Edmond smiled at his sister.

"'This news comes as a shock to the nation but not to his friend, Dr. Watson who confirmed he knew about them but was sworn to secrecy. He has indicated he is looking forward to getting to know his friend's family better. Sherlock Holmes has confirmed he will still be taking cases in his private capacity until further notice.'" Edmond finished reading and looked over the newspaper at his family as he reached for a glass of wine at his elbow.

"Devilishly handsome?" Charles, Percy to his family, quoted sitting opposite his brother in Dr. Watson's old armchair, smoking a cigarette while nursing a glass of wine. "I have been called many things, *mon père*, but never devilishly handsome."

"Clearly a fact attributed to your mother," Holmes answered with a smirk as he stood in front of the fire with his cigarette in one hand and whisky-soda in the other.

"How long do you think it'll be before we stop being newsworthy, papa?" Rebecca asked from her seat next to her mother on the chaise lounge.

"I do not know, my dear," he answered. "I only did just announce you yesterday. I'm sure it will take the London papers longer than that and the criminal classes have been decidedly dull recently so there has been no murder to take your place on the front page. You are all right with this whole thing, aren't you?" Holmes asked. When he proposed the idea to his family the last time he went to France they all seemed prepared for it. But, seeing the concern on his daughter's face, he was worried the stress of being sensational news could be taking its toll on her.

"I admit I feel a little conspicuous when people stand outside the flat trying to get a glimpse of us," she answered. "But *oui*, I am more than all right with this, papa. It is a dream come true to be here with you and meeting Dr. Watson. I suppose I did not realize it would be such earth shattering news."

"Becca, you know the reason I kept you all in France, I was sure someone would try and use you to get to me and I couldn't put you all in that sort of danger. We all agreed to reveal our secret, but I would spare you this if I could, my sweet one." Holmes explained.

"I do understand, papa, and I appreciate all you and mama did," she answered. "But I am not a child and I knew the newspapers would be interested in selling papers. My only concern is, how am I to know a proper suitor from the ones only interested in my name."

"You have us," Edmond replied handing his brother the newspaper at Percy's beckoning.

"Thank you, Edmond," Rebecca smiled at her elder brother. "I am being silly."

"Not at all, it is a legitimate concern," Edmond stated. "But believe me when I tell you, we would never let anyone take advantage of you. You have my word, as your brother."

"*Je t'aime, mon frère*," she blew him a small kiss. He caught it and held his closed fist to his heart and winked something they had done since they were children.

"I believe the fact a man of your standing, father, a confirmed bachelor as it were, having a wife and children of all things is such a sensational bit of knowledge, books may be written about us for years to come," Percy replied.

"If Watson doesn't beat them all to it," Holmes answered.

"Where is the good doctor?" Marguerite stood and walked over to her husband. "We haven't seen him all day."

"He told me he would be staying at his flat; he didn't want to intrude on our time together. You all just finished unpacking. Are you boys finding your arrangements suitable?" Holmes asked.

Percy and Edmond nodded.

"I am enjoying my time at Uncle's flat in Pall Mall," Edmond replied.

"I am afraid I will be moving out of Uncle's flat very soon. I ran into Cedric earlier today. He had seen the paper and was thrilled to see me. I did not realize he was in London, but he was at the tea shop this morning. He offered a room at his flat. I will be moving my things there tomorrow," Percy said.

"I did not realize Cedric was here either," Holmes answered. "Last I heard he was still in Paris."

"He asked after you all and wished to come and greet you properly but was unsure if you were available. I invited him to dinner tomorrow night. If that is well with you, mama," Percy explained.

"Of course," Marguerite gushed. "Cedric is like family. It has been too long since we have seen him. Did he look well?"

"He is very well," Percy answered. "He was very happy for us to finally be here."

"Cedric is so dear," Rebecca said softly. "I remember when he came home with you both from school. We all had such fun times together. I am sure he only remembers me as an annoying young girl."

"Nonsense," Percy looked up at Holmes and Marguerite for a moment sharing a secret. "He asked after you specifically, Becs."

"Truly?" she asked.

"Perhaps you could wear that beautiful maroon gown we purchased in Paris, *ma cherie*," Marguerite said. "For dinner tomorrow."

Rebecca nodded enthusiastically and again Percy glanced up at Holmes and Marguerite.

"Watson did ask us to his lodgings for a dinner engagement this week, my dear, if you are available," Holmes said when Marguerite turned to pour another glass of wine for Percy and Edmond.

"Oh well, I'll have to let the queen know I cannot have tea," she teased as she passed the glasses to her sons. After their thanks, she continued. "Of course, I would love to."

"Tell us Sir, you were working a case? I believe the

article mentioned something about a criminal act worthy of Jack the Ripper?" Edmond asked.

"It did have some interesting characteristics," Holmes admitted. "But Watson would ask I wait to say anything until after the Strand has run its first copies."

"Then it's off to Northern England for a bit of a reprieve from all of this," Marguerite answered sitting next to her daughter.

"You will love Mycroft's estate near there. He has offered it as a location for your ball, my dear," Holmes said to his daughter.

"That is very kind of him," she said.

"Well," Marguerite sighed. "It is extremely late, perhaps Rebecca and I will retire and leave the three of you in peace."

"I actually should be getting back," Percy said standing and adjusting his waistcoat.

"I'm right behind you," Edmond replied. "I am rather tired myself."

"You do not have to go," Marguerite said.

"Mother, it is after midnight and after the excitement of this week I feel like a hollow shell of myself," Percy stated.

"And you look it," Edmond teased.

Percy chuckled. "Goodnight," he wished his family.

Rebecca wished her parents a good night and headed up the stairs to Dr. Watson's old room. When they were alone, Marguerite turned to her husband.

"What is it, Sherlock? What has you worried?" She asked.

He turned toward the fire. "This whole thing, Margot. It is a dream come true, but I cannot stop thinking. Wondering. Worrying. What if? There are things in the shadows, they know most of it, yes but what about the others? With my past? How long is this euphoria to last? How long until my past with all its secrets and shadows rears its head? I wonder if this is right."

Marguerite laid a comforting hand on the small of his back.

"They are grown, *mon cher*. We worry of course, we are their parents. But they all know the risks. Why do you think Edmond has taught us all how to defend ourselves? Or Percy always carries his swordstick? Or Rebecca has her revolver in her handbag and a knife in her stocking. We all know the risks, Sherlock. And yes, you live a dangerous lifestyle, but would they be any safer if you were Prime Minister? I doubt it. Release that burden, my love. It does nothing."

Holmes nodded but was silent for a time. "You are correct as usual, Margot. And dear god never say if I was Prime Minister, please. I would die of boredom."

Marguerite laughed but slid her hand down his arm to his hand and intertwined their fingers.

"Come to bed, Sherlock Holmes. We will not think on that anymore."

Draining his drink, he nodded and followed his wife to their room.

Chapter Four

The man hurried through the alley, jumping at the sounds around him. He found the correct number, reached up and knocked on the door. When the door finally opened he said the pass phrase and was granted entry. He was led into a darkened room where the only light was a single candle on a table. The man he was there to see, sat in the arm chair beside the table reading a book by the light.

"What is it?" the man asked in an annoyed tone.

"I was told you needed someone for a very specific objective," he answered. The man looked up, but his face was too shadowed to see anything. Closing the book slowly, the man observed him.

"Yes, I think you'll do nicely," the man said. "Tell me, lad, have you stolen anything before?"

"There's a first time for everything," he answered.

Rebecca placed the last piece of her brown hair just as

the bell at the door rang. Cedric was there. She stood and gazed at her reflection in the mirror. The beautiful maroon silk hugged her bodice and flowed from her hips. Overlaid with a paisley pattern of gold and maroon, the outer layer matched the sleeves. Her mother, stanchly against the corset for any occasion never insisted her daughter wear one. Rebecca thanked her mother's looks as she gazed at her silhouette. The rare moments she counted herself pretty she could count on one hand but as she looked at the debutante in the mirror, she smiled. A knock at her bedroom door drew her attention. Calling for her mother to enter, Rebecca stood back so Marguerite could see her.

"Oh my darling," she breathed. "How stunning you look."

"I confess I am so nervous, mama," she said. "I... I do not want to let either you or papa down, but I fear I may as soon as I see Cedric."

"You have always cared for him even as a young girl."

"I have," she looked down.

"Do you still?"

"I do not know him yet. The man he has become is a stranger."

"He is still our Cedric," Marguerite replied walking closer to her daughter and taking her hands. "You be who you are. Anything else would let your father and I down."

"What if I choose the wrong fork or spill my wine?" she gazed into her mother's eyes.

"Then laugh, and smile, and let it go," Marguerite replied. "You are not perfect, my love. Do not hold yourself to that measurement. Now I know what it is like to be nervous when you are to see someone... a man... you care for. But your father and I and your brothers are here. And we love you and when Cedric sees you in that gown... he's the one who will use the wrong fork and spill his wine." Marguerite giggled at Rebecca's embarrassed smile. "Now, he is here, come down, my love."

Rebecca nodded and took her mother's hand. Together they walked down the stairs hearing the men's voices.

"Cedric, my lord it is good to see you," Holmes shook the man's hand.

"It is wonderful to see you too, Mr. Holmes. When I saw the announcement in the newspaper I wanted to come and see you but I also wanted to give everyone a chance to settle before," the twenty-five year old stated.

"It has been years," Holmes said. "When did you move back to London?"

"But three years ago," he answered. "My brother is not in good health."

"I am sorry," Holmes replied. "But you should have come see me."

"I wanted to, many times," Cedric admitted. "I missed everyone but I was unsure how it would be received. I knew Dr. Watson was still staying here on occasion. How did I explain our relationship without slipping up?"

"Watson knows no French," Holmes laughed. "But I am glad you are here now. Percy kept me informed of your progress through your letters to him."

"I am glad," Cedric answered. "London is a lonely place and so unlike the French countryside. I do miss it."

"As we all do," Edmond replied handing him a glass of wine. "But it is good to be together again."

"Thank you and indeed, I have missed you all. Oh, Percy, I meant to tell you, do you remember Sir Reginald Hardy?"

"Hardy, Hardy... ah yes, the club," Percy nodded remembering someone he had met once in passing the other day.

"He has invited us to dinner Friday," Cedric said. "Shall I tell him we will both be there?"

"Sounds excellent," Percy replied. "I would be delighted."

"Good," Cedric replied. "I would have invited you as well, Edmond, but I know how much you detest social dinners."

"You know me well," Edmond raised his glass of wine

toward him.

"Thank you for having me to dine tonight, Mr. Holmes," he said.

"You are always welcome," he answered.

"Do forgive me for being a little late I was in conference with my brother's solicitors."

"Is all well?"

"I hope so," Cedric said. "Gérard has not been handling the funds correctly and they came to me in accordance with my father's will. My father wrote it that if they deemed his actions to be detrimental to the Somers' name I would be given power of the finances over my brother. They have invoked that portion of my father's will. I had to sign some papers. They were longwinded, and I did not want to sign them but my hand was forced. We were running over our meeting. I do apologize and hope I have not kept you waiting."

"Not at all," Holmes answered. "Rebecca is still upstairs. It will be the first time you have seen Rebecca in nearly five years."

"Indeed, she was a lovely young girl when last I met her," Cedric replied.

"Well, she's nearly eighteen now," Percy stated. "Hardly a girl any longer."

The door opened and Marguerite walked in, her eyes immediately going to Cedric.

"Dear Cedric!" she cried greeting him with two kisses on the cheeks. "It has been too long."

"Good evening, *madame*," he said. "You look lovely, as ever."

"Oh, you may be English through and through, but you will always have a bit of the Frenchman in you," she teased.

"According to my accent, no one would believe I am English," he answered.

Rebecca announced herself by clearing her throat gently. All eyes turned to her but Cedric's reaction was all she cared to see. His face froze but soon his jaw dropped and he blinked a couple times.

"*Bonsoir*, Cedric," she said. "It is good to see you."

Cedric said nothing, could say nothing for a moment,

until a strangled laugh slipped out of his throat. "Rebecca?" he questioned. "Dear god, last I saw you, you were a child."

"I was twelve," she replied. "I am not twelve any longer."

He shook his head dumbfounded. "You are stunning."

Her smile caused a shiver to race down his spine. Then he remembered he was in the midst of her family, her two older brothers and her father to be specific, and he snapped out of his surprise.

"Forgive me," he walked over to her and took her hand in his, kissing her fingertips. "You look beautiful, Miss Holmes."

"Oh please, Cedric, we are friends are we not?" she asked. "Please call me Rebecca as you always have done."

"Perhaps not the best," he admitted, his gazed drifting back to Holmes and Marguerite. "You are to be presented and I am a bachelor. We are not related."

"You may use her Christian name when we are alone, Cedric," Holmes gave his permission. "And Rebecca, you know this already, my dear but he is Sir Cedric whenever, if ever you are out in mixed company."

"Of course," she nodded. "How is your brother?"

"Fine," he replied still letting the shock of seeing her wear off. "Uh... he's ill but he is... fine."

"I am so sorry," she said. "Do give Baron Hughes our best."

"I will," he stated.

"Rebecca, dear," her mother called to her. "Wine?"

"Thank you, mama," she smiled at her mother.

"Dinner will be served soon. Perhaps we can all sit down?" Marguerite offered. Percy and Edmond watched Cedric but said nothing as they offered the ladies a seat and stood together before the fire.

Chapter Five

Sherlock Holmes and Marguerite were greeted by Dr. Watson's housekeeper. She took Marguerite's fur wrap and Holmes' topcoat.

"Mr. Holmes," he heard a voice call. Looking up he saw Alexandra Watson at the top of the stairs. "It is so very good to see you again." She rushed down to him.

He took her hand in a tender greeting. "Alexandra, please allow me to present my wife, Marguerite," he said. Alexandra smiled brightly at her and kissed her cheeks.

"Papa has spoken of you," she replied. "Please, come up. We are all very pleased you were able to make it."

Alexandra turned and led them up the stairs. Marguerite spoke low and in her native language to her husband.

"Who is she?" she asked.

"Watson's daughter," Holmes answered.

"I did not realize he had one," she replied.

"His first wife in Afghanistan," Holmes explained. "Alexandra was born there. Her mother died and she was sent to London. That was one reason he married Mary Morsten. Alexandra needed a mother. He told me about her when we first met but his writings had no need to mention her since she was never involved in our cases. But I have met her before."

"What age is she?" Marguerite asked.

"Twenty," he answered.

"Has she been presented?" Marguerite asked.

"Yes," Holmes answered.

"Is she not married?"

"No," Holmes answered. Marguerite nodded slowly but said nothing for a moment.

"Percy or Edmond?" she asked.

Holmes looked down at his wife trying and failing to suppress his grin.

"Why, Mrs. Holmes, whatever do you mean?" he teased back to English.

"Oh, come now, Sherlock," she replied. "She is quite a lovely young lady."

"Percy, I do believe," he answered.

"I agree," Marguerite said giving his hand a squeeze as they reached the top of the stairwell.

"Holmes, good to see you, old chap," Watson greeted him jovially as they entered the room.

Holmes set his teacup down as he sat in Baker Street late Friday afternoon. His eyes roved the newspaper. He was fooling no one. As much as he loved his family and as many times as he had told Marguerite it was only with her he was able to calm his mind, they all knew he was bored.

"Anything interesting in the paper, Sherlock?" Marguerite asked.

He merely grunted. Marguerite shook her head when her sons looked at her. Rebecca sat beside her and covered a grin.

"Papa?" Rebecca said softly. Holmes didn't answer but she continued. "This article here," she indicated the one facing her. Holmes flipped the newspaper over. "What is it?"

"Boring," Sherlock replied. Rebecca laughed lightly.

"Perhaps it could be interesting?" Marguerite asked.

"Doubtful," Holmes answered.

It was several minutes later when Holmes closed the newspaper with a huff, grabbed up his tea cup and drained it. He looked up at his children and leaned back in the chair.

"Your mother and I have tickets to see Don Giovanni tonight," he announced.

"That should be interesting," Percy replied.

"I am looking forward to it," Marguerite stated. "Finally, be able to go to the opera with my husband. The looks and whispers will be well accepted now," she teased. "What about you Percy?"

"One of Cedric's friends has invited us both to dine with him this evening. So I shall be with him," Percy replied. "I'm afraid the looks and whispers will have to wait for me, mama."

"And you Edmond?" Holmes asked.

"Uncle Mycroft has asked me to dinner," Edmond replied. "I do not know if it is anything of note."

"Do you have anything fashionable to wear?" His brother teased. "You are the less fashionable one," he winked.

"Just because I am more comfortable without shirt and shoes and outside among nature does not mean I do not know how to dress, *mon frère*. My overtly fashion-conscious brother has taught me well enough," Edmond ribbed.

"Oh lord," Percy taunted. "Better take my second-best dinner attire."

"I am not sure how it would fit me," Edmond said eyeing his brother and then looking at his physique. Though Percy was by no means a small man, Edmond's back alone would rip the seams of Percy's dinner coat if he so much as shrugged his shoulders.

"Have you forgotten we exchanged clothes all the time in France?" Percy asked.

"Exchanged? No, I have not forgotten how you tried to force me into fashionable collars and neckties," Edmond goaded.

Percy huffed a sigh. "All my efforts are for naught."

"Well, you will be happy to know you will not be alone

tonight, Rebecca," Marguerite said. "Miss Alexandra Watson has asked to come over and spend time with you."

"Indeed?" Rebecca beamed. "I do enjoy her company."

"Who?" Percy asked.

"Oh, that's right I forgot you have not met her," Marguerite said. "The good doctor's daughter from his first wife in Afghanistan, Alexandra Watson."

"I had no idea the doctor had a daughter," Percy replied.

"Oh yes," Holmes answered. "Watson did not want all of England to know of her; the same way I did not want them to know about all of you. He kept her out of the fiction he wrote of me."

Marguerite stopped pouring her husband's refill of tea.

"Fiction?" she asked. "You forget I have been married to you for twenty-five years, my love, he has captured you quite well on the page."

Holmes looked over at her sardonically. "Thank you, my dear," he answered.

"What is her age?" Percy asked.

"Twenty," Holmes answered. Percy snuffed out the cigarette he held between his fingers.

"Is she... interesting?" Percy asked.

"She is extremely beautiful," Rebecca answered her brother's interested reaction.

"Yes, indeed," Marguerite replied. "You must meet her yourself to answer your question of interesting."

"Just understand," Holmes started. "This is all new. I want you all to be careful, especially you Rebecca. Remember I have been involved in numerous cases and put several criminals away. Percy, Edmond, Rebecca, just promise me you all will be conscious of your surroundings."

"Of course," Edmond said. "Have no fear, father."

"My only fear is that this is not France, it is London," Holmes replied. "Take nothing for granted. Be on your guard. No one really knows what or who is lurking in the shadows."

Chapter Six

"Welcome, Miss Watson," Marguerite spoke to the doctor's daughter. "It is good to see you again."

"Thank you, Mrs. Holmes," she answered. "It is good to see you. I hope you are well."

"Very well, thank you, my dear," Marguerite said.

"Your gown is lovely," Alexandra complimented.

"Oh, thank you. Mr. Holmes and I are going to the opera," she replied. "We are all out tonight, I'm afraid, which is why I was very glad to have received your letter. Rebecca would have been so lonely." Turning to the stairs, Marguerite called softly up to her daughter. "Becca has been staying in your father's old room. Dr. Watson helped her move all of his furniture out and got the place ready for her."

"Papa is quite taken with her," Alexandra replied. "He says she is the prettiest little thing and he will be fourth in line whenever a young man shows an interest. If the man gets past Mr. Holmes' and your sons' scrutiny, Papa will be the last line of defense, and god help them if they get to him, he says. He keeps saying he was a soldier and I keep reminding him he was a doctor."

Both women giggled.

"He is a wonderful gentleman and I am very grateful to him for keeping Sherlock grounded while he was away from us," Marguerite said. "He can be a handful even for me. But like his sons, he is quite worth the challenge."

"I have yet to have the pleasure of meeting your sons, Mrs. Holmes," she said.

"Oh, they will certainly be around and we will have to remedy that as quickly as possible," Marguerite promised. "You have already met Cedric, though have you not?"

Alexandra blushed slightly and looked down.

"I did not realize you knew him. He is not one of your sons," she questioned.

"As good as," Marguerite answered. "He and my sons Charles and Edmond grew up together. He is such a dear man, isn't he?"

"Indeed," she answered. "He is a good man too." Before Marguerite could pry anymore as to the nature of their relationship, Rebecca appeared at the top of the stairs.

After the two young ladies exchanged pleasantries, they moved into the study and sat down near the fire. Holmes came up the stairs.

"The cab is here, my dear," he called to his wife. "And Percy forgot his cigarette case this afternoon." Holmes entered the room followed by Percy. The women stood and Alexandra's eyes went immediately to Percy's. Marguerite stepped forward.

"Allow me, Miss Watson to introduce my eldest son, Charles," she said.

"Percy," Percy corrected with his nickname and middle name.

"Of course," Marguerite smiled and sent a knowing glance at her husband. "Percy, this is Miss Watson," his mother said.

"Alexandra," she corrected. Percy smirked. "A pleasure," she answered.

"One that is all mine," he replied.

At opera house, her arm through Sherlock's, Marguerite walked confidently through the lobby toward a secluded space near the doors of the auditorium. Sherlock left her alone for a moment as he went to get some refreshment. Marguerite took it all in. The beauty of the opera house was unrivaled, except perhaps by the one in Paris.

As it was one of their first public appearances, the scrutiny was fierce. Marguerite felt the eyes of every person on her. Accepting their curiosity as a part of the circumstances, Marguerite plastered a smile on her lips as she waited for Sherlock to return with flutes of champagne.

"I say, Hardy, what was in that wine?" Cedric yawned as he accepted his cards in the drawing room.

"Nothing but grapes and fermentation, old chap,"

Reginald Hardy replied dealing the game. "Though I must admit to be feeling a bit sluggish myself. Spooner, are you that desperate to win?"

"Hardly gents with the way you've both been playing," Harry Spooner answered. "I need little aid."

"Damn right," Reginald replied covering a yawn. "I say, that is odd." He shook his head violently trying to clear it. "Where is that friend of yours, Somers?" Hardy asked looking at his cards.

"Yes, I was rather looking forward to meeting Sherlock Holmes' son," Spooner said.

"All I know is he was heading to his father's flat and if he was not back in twenty minutes I was to go on without him," Cedric replied.

"No matter," Spooner answered. "Probably got distracted by some pretty face, eh?"

"Whatever did happen between you and Miss Watson, old chap?" Hardy asked. "I thought for sure there were wedding bells in your future."

"No such attachment I assure you," Cedric said. "She is a charming lady and I was very taken by her. She's far too good for you rogues, that's for sure."

"Got your eye on another?" Hardy asked.

"I am distracted with my brother's illness," Cedric answered. "I was not ready to marry and the only honorable thing to do after the few weeks we courted was to release her from any impropriety."

"Honorable, eh?" Hardy asked chuckling. "You can't deny what you told me that evening."

"A gentleman would never reveal what his friend told him in a drunken moment," Cedric's eyes bored into him.

"Oh, this sounds interesting," Spooner said.

"It is," Hardy answered. "They were caught in a passionate embrace by her father."

"Indeed?" Spooner raised his eyebrows.

"It was nothing of the sort and you know it, Hardy," Cedric replied. "I'll not have you slandering the poor girl. I asked for a kiss that is all. She agreed and we were engaged thusly when her father entered the room. He was angered I would behave in such a cavalier manner and asked me to leave and to never see her again. Luckily, we were able to make the break, as they say, cleanly."

"Did she not kiss well?" Spooner asked.

"That is not something you should even ask me," Cedric replied.

"I know..." Spooner said. "But did she?"

Cedric sighed knowing they would not move on from the subject until he replied.

"If you must know," he answered. "It was her first kiss."

Chapter Seven

The opera was excellent and during the intermission Holmes and Marguerite stood close whispering to each other.

"Well, my love?" Holmes asked. "What think you of the evening?"

"Rather entertaining," she answered. "Who knew the English would be such an interesting people? I find it hard to concentrate on the performance."

Holmes raised his whisky to his lips and gazed at his wife over the rim of the glass. Once he took a swallow, he studied her.

"Surely you do not mean the woman who is staring at you in the borrowed dress and ill-fitting shoes who has an affinity to all things fine except for her gambling husband."

"No of course not, she is merely looking at you, trying to see if I would be an easy woman to get around," she answered. "She is looking for the next in a long stream of lovers." Marguerite took a sip of her wine.

"Well, no worry on that, my love," Holmes replied. "I am a well satisfied married man. My eyes would not roam."

"Of course," Marguerite shrugged. "You know no woman would be able to put up with you as I do."

Holmes' lips quirked up into a grin. "Minx."

She did not reply but a playful glint entered her eye.

"Well, well, Holmes is this your lovely wife?" A voice behind Marguerite made her turn. She looked up into the eyes of a well-dressed man with bushy side-whiskers and a jovial smile.

"Yes, indeed, Prime Minister," Holmes answered. "Mrs. Holmes, may I introduce to you the Premier."

Marguerite greeted him and offered her hand to him. The PM kissed her gloved fingers.

"It is a pleasure to meet such a lovely lady," he said.

"Oh, thank you, my lord," she replied. "It is a pleasure to be back in my father's homeland."

"You grew up in Yorkshire, I believe I read."

"I lived there for a time," she answered. "And met Mr. Holmes there. But France was my mother's homeland."

"Did you live with your mother?"

"No, she passed many years before when I was a young girl. My father's estate is in Yorkshire and when Mr. Holmes and I married we moved back to France."

"I see. Well, I am looking forward to meeting the rest of your family. Your sons are gentlemen?" The Prime Minister asked.

"They are, with an income from my mother," Holmes explained.

"Excellent," he replied. "And I am greatly looking forward to meeting your daughter. If she is half as beautiful as her mother, the young men will not know what to do with themselves."

"She will be presented this season, my lord," Marguerite said.

"Splendid, splendid. I must say you could have knocked me down with a feather when I read the morning's post that day. But why on earth would you keep this gorgeous creature a secret for so long, Holmes? It's not as if you could possibly be ashamed. And I know all of England would not have viewed you any differently."

"I had my reasons, my lord," Holmes answered. The bell rang indicating the second act was starting. The audience turned as one and began heading into the auditorium.

"I say, Holmes," the Prime Minister called to him. Holmes looked back at him. "The paper said you would still be accepting cases in your official capacity for a time, is that true?" He asked.

"I am still at your service, Sir," Holmes replied.

"Good," he answered. The PM smiled slightly and walked away from them.

Marguerite turned to her husband.

"Expect the PM tonight, I see," she said.

"Quiet so," he raised her fingers to his lips. "Do you desire to see the second half? Or would you prefer to join me for... other entertainment back at Baker Street?"

"Why, Mr. Holmes, I thought you would never ask," she answered.

Holmes turned to help his wife out of the cab as it came to a stop outside of 221B Baker Street. Holmes quickly unlocked the door and led his wife inside. Marguerite stood waiting for him as he shut and locked the door behind him. Taking off her fur wrap and hat, she set them on the hallway stand. Holmes turned to her as she stepped into him. Without words, she reached up and took his hat off, unbuttoned his coat and slid it from his shoulders. He stood watching her as she worked. Coming around to stand in front of him again, Marguerite set his coat and hat beside hers.

Slipping his arm around her waist he pulled her to him and pressed his lips to hers. Marguerite responded as she always did. Her arms around his neck, she pressed her body close to his. Her fingernails scratching his scalp, she muffled his soft groan. She pulled back far too quickly, but said nothing, only raised his hand in hers and turned, leading him up the stairs.

Though, just as they were about to enter their room, laughter rang out from the study. Exchanging looks, they righted their clothing and opened the door to see Rebecca, Alexandra and Percy seated close together.

"Ah, good evening, Father, Mother, was the opera not to your liking?" Percy asked.

"No, it was wonderful, I was merely tired," Marguerite replied.

"Didn't you have a dinner engagement tonight, Percy?" Holmes annoyed voice caused Marguerite to subtly pinch his arm.

"Indeed, I did," Percy answered with a smirk as he watched them. Marguerite's cheeks were flushed, and Holmes' stance was impatient. It would not be the first time Percy interrupted their time together. "But we all got to talking and with Alexandra's charming conversation, I'm afraid time slipped away. I am sure my friends will forgive me."

"Your son was regaling us with some very insightful observations," Alexandra explained.

"Some little deductions my father taught me," Percy smiled.

"Showing off again, Percy?" Marguerite asked, stepping further into the room much to Sherlock's chagrin.

"Always, Mother," their son replied.

"Well," Holmes started, coming up and slipping his arm around Marguerite. "You're welcome to stay as long as you would like, Alexandra."

"Thank you, Mr. Holmes, but I think I should be going. It was such a wonderful evening. Thank you both for your stimulating conversation." She looked at Percy and Rebecca.

"Our pleasure, Miss Watson," Rebecca said.

"Alexandra, my dear, please," she asked.

"Allow me to see you home, Alexandra," Percy offered.

"Thank you," she replied. They headed to the door and Percy helped her into her coat and took his top coat. After their good nights were said, Rebecca went up to her room leaving Holmes and Marguerite alone. Again, Marguerite said nothing, only looked up at her husband and walked toward their room. Holmes followed and shut the door behind them.

Chapter Eight

A knock at his door stirred Holmes from his light doze. He looked over then down at Marguerite, her head lay on his shoulder, as she outlined a bullet scar on his chest.

"Who is it?" Holmes called.

"It's me, sir," Holmes recognized Mrs. Hudson's voice.

"A moment, Mrs. Hudson," he said, checking to make sure they were covered as Marguerite moved to lie on her side of the bed. "Come in."

The door opened and Mrs. Hudson walked over, wringing her hands.

"Oh, sir," she said.

"Well, Mrs. Hudson, what is it?" He asked.

"I'm sorry to bother you, sir, but it's the Prime Minister, sir," she said.

Holmes and Marguerite looked at each other.

"He's late," they said together.

"Ah, Prime Minister, forgive me for keeping you waiting. My wife and I retired just after we returned home," Holmes came out of his room and addressed the PM.

"I looked for you after the opera ended but did not find you," he said.

"Ah, yes, forgive us, my wife had a headache," Holmes said heading to the fireplace and the box of cigarettes. "Mrs. Holmes begs your pardon, she has retired."

"Of course, I would never intrude if it were not absolutely essential to speak with you," he said. Holmes lit a cigarette.

"You need have no concern on that account, my lord. I am used to being needed at all hours of the day," Holmes offered the chair behind the PM. He sat, and Holmes went over to the side board, pouring two glasses of whisky and soda.

"Oh, thank you very much, Mr. Holmes," the Prime Minister said accepting the drink and a cigarette from Holmes' case.

"Now, my lord, how about you tell me more about the affair at Whitehall and what it was there that caused you to come to me in such a hurry?" Holmes sat down across from him.

"How do you know that?" The PM asked.

"I will not bore you with my methods, but it is clear clay on your shoes is fresh from today. You haven't had a chance to change your evening clothes since the opera. So clearly you have not been home. Where did you go in these two hours between the opera and now? Well, something must have happened at Whitehall for you to ask to consult me, but it was not so urgent. You waited to come to me after the opera. Therefore, this visit initially was to be a consult for advice. Something must have happened to make this a consult for help as your appearance would notate."

"I suppose I should not be surprised after having known your brother for any length of time," the PM replied. "Well then, I'll get to the facts."

Holmes said nothing, only puffed on his cigarette and waited. The PM stood and walked to the window.

"Do you know of the Rebellion going on in China for the

past year?" The PM started.

"My lord, I make it a rule to never fill my head with any rubbish that is not essential to my current investigations," Holmes lied. Edmond kept him up to date on all the current events in the Orient as he had studied in China for eight years. The rebellion was, in fact a topic of great discussion between them.

"Of course," The PM said. "Well, The Boxer Rebellion, as the papers have dubbed it, is currently the cause of panic among the British people. In the past, you have been very good to help us discretely with some important inquires. I must ask, no… implore you to assist in this case."

"A moment, Sir, you have yet to tell me what has happened," Holmes said.

"Of course, forgive me. You are absolutely right, Mr. Holmes, I did plan on coming to you earlier tonight, but I received this letter just after the final curtain fell at Don Giovanni." He produced a folded piece of paper from his inside breast pocket. He walked over to Holmes and handed him the letter.

"'The Boxers," Holmes read. "'Don't like secrets, and you've been keeping secrets from us. We will take them back tonight. Expect a certain document to be missing from Whitehall after the opera!' Hmm…"

"I rushed to our agent's house in Whitehall to find the place burgled and our agent was drugged. The document he was protecting was gone," the PM explained.

Holmes observed the paper.

"Written on plain note paper, torn from a booklet. The writer is clearly male from the angle and style of writing, but hurried. There's evidence they wrote this note in a short span of time. Perhaps they were worried about being found out… The pen was a soft nosed tip, little help there…" Holmes sniffed the paper. "Hmm, he smokes heavily… Cherrywood… he also drinks but not as much as he smokes. A youngish man, good status in society, trying heavily to make it appear he's a foreigner… perhaps they're holding something over him… debts maybe? Family member? Hmm…" he looked up at the PM's face. "So sorry, Prime Minister, please go on. You were telling me about the document that went missing."

"I've utilized your talents so often, I was expecting that question," the PM shook himself from his stunned stupor and continued. "Even so, I must ask you for your word as a gentleman and an Englishman, you will keep the information to yourself."

"You have it," Holmes said.

"Very well," the PM replied sitting opposite Holmes. "This document outlined the—"

"*Père, es-tu ici?*" A voice said as someone knocked sharply on the door.

Holmes stood and opened the door to his son. "Come in, Percy."

"Oh, forgive me, sir, I did not know you had a visitor," Percy said. His eyes lighted on the PM and he pulled himself up to his full height. "Prime Minister, it is an honor," he bowed slightly.

"My lord," Holmes stood. "Allow me to introduce my eldest, Charles Holmes."

"Pleasure," the PM replied.

"Did you escort Miss Watson home?" Holmes asked.

"Yes, sir," Percy answered. "She and the good doctor invited me for a sherry before I left. I just came over here on my way to Cedric's."

"Excellent, sit down," Holmes said. "I may need your help."

"Mr. Holmes, I must protest," the PM said heatedly. "You and your brother I know, but as much as I respect you, this is a matter of England's security. I do not mean to cause offense, but I do not know your son."

"My lord, I assure you Charles is discretion itself. It would be no different than having the good doctor with me only my son has more experience in analytical deduction."

"Even so," the PM stated. "I'm afraid I must protest. This is not something a French-"

"My lord," Holmes stopped him with a harsh snap. "I must request you remember you are in my home and you are speaking to my son. If you insult him, you insult me, and I will ask you to leave."

Percy looked at his father and blinked. He never meant for his presence to cause a problem.

"Whatever is said here, my lord would never be repeated," Percy said. "If you would prefer, I will leave."

"My son has worked on several cases with me, my lord," Holmes explained. "He is completely trustworthy."

"I see," the PM stated. "Well, then, perhaps it would be beneficial to have you on this case, Mr. Holmes."

Percy smiled slightly and sat in the empty seat. Holmes handed him the letter and the PM explained the case.

"May I ask who this agent is?" Percy asked when the PM was finished.

"That I'm afraid is not in my power to reveal, even to your father," the PM said.

"My lord," Holmes interjected sarcastically, reminding him of his methods.

"Fine," he answered sighing. "The Home Office agent was Sir Reginald Hardy, son of the prominent Parliamentary member Lord Michael Beckett."

"Sir Reginald?" Percy started surprised.

"The man you were to meet tonight, Percy," Holmes stated.

"Indeed, we were to have dinner tonight. Hardy, Cedric and myself. Was he injured?" Percy asked.

"No, just drugged," the PM replied. "But the document outlining the British war ships off the coast of Japan was stolen. If the Boxers get hold of such a document it could mean the end of Britain's involvement in the war and thousands, even millions of pounds may be lost."

"Not to mention the considerable loss of life to the men aboard those ships," Percy said.

"Well, of course there is that," the PM replied.

"Well then there is not a moment to lose. Let us go," Holmes went back to his room to retrieve his coat and they heard him speaking to Marguerite. Once he was properly attired, the three men left the flat.

Chapter
Nine

As the Prime Minister's carriage rattled through the foggy streets of London, Percy turned to his father and spoke low.

"What do you think could be the purpose for stealing the document? Blackmail of someone close to him? Part of a larger plot to destroy the empire?" Percy asked.

"All valid ideas, but what makes you think it's anything more than a simple robbery or a specific robbery for that document?" Holmes asked. "Why does it have to be a part of a larger plan?"

"Was anything else stolen, my lord?" Percy asked. The PM shook his head. "That fact alone, Sir would indicate this was not a random robbery," Percy explained to his father.

"Good, what else?" Holmes asked.

Percy looked at his father's profile and sighed. "My respect for the good doctor has grown exponentially," he grumbled. Holmes chuckled. "Could you not just tell me?"

"I could, but why, when you know already?" Holmes asked.

"The fact Sir Reginald was not injured indicates it could have been someone he knew who wanted him out of the way but not harmed." Percy said.

"Good," Holmes replied. "What makes you think the Boxers are not a part of it?"

"Whitehall is a very elegant section of town, an Oriental man would have been suspicious in such an area," Percy went on. "And I take it no such person was reported to have been sighted."

"Wonderful," Holmes complimented. "Really, Percy, most wonderful. Now we will be able to test your theory very soon if I'm not mistaken."

Percy looked out of the cab window and saw the house come into view. The police presence outside was not subtle at all. The Prime Minister's carriage rolled to a stop and they filed out.

"Hmm," Holmes said his brow furrowed. "It is most unfortunate the police arrived before I did. Who knows how much evidence they trampled over in the short time they've been here."

Percy laughed outright. "How many times have I read about you saying the same thing to Watson?"

"They are like a herd of cattle and about as intelligent as one too," Holmes grumbled.

They walked into the house and were greeted by a ruddy faced man in his mid-thirties.

"Mr. Holmes," he greeted him.

"Good evening, Gregson," Holmes replied.

"Inspector Gregson?" Percy breathed. The man looked at him questioningly. "I have read about you. It is so good to finally meet you."

"Aye, and you," he replied but turned back to Holmes. "New companion, Holmes? Whatever happened to Dr. Watson?"

"This is my son, Gregson," Holmes replied.

"Your what?" Gregson asked. "Oh, that's a laugh, Mr. Holmes. But whatever this young man is to you," he winked suggestively. "I hope the good doctor is aware."

"Keenly," Holmes ground out.

"It is clear you do not read the papers, inspector," Percy began. "Honestly, it is refreshing to meet someone who does not. Rest assured, I am Sherlock Holmes' son but since it is clear you are just as intelligent as you appear and as Dr. Watson wrote you, perhaps it would be best to table this conversation and speak on more pressing matters such as the missing document and the safety of England."

Holmes looked expectantly at Gregson.

"Everything is just as we found it," Gregson answered. "We received your instructions and made sure the scene was preserved."

"My instructions?" Holmes asked surprised. "I sent you no message."

"No, sir, no written note," Gregson answered.

"Then what did you receive?" He asked.

"Your messenger, he's waiting for you in the room. If you'll follow me," Gregson led the three of them towards the closed door.

When the door opened, Holmes saw his brother standing near the safe. Edmond was crouched low gazing at the lock, his back to them.

"Hello, Mycroft," Holmes said. "What on earth are you doing here?"

"This is a matter of national security, Sherlock, of course I'm here. I very much despair at ever getting back to my usual routine." Mycroft said.

"Perhaps that is my fault, sir," Edmond stood and turned to them. Holmes greeting his son.

"Edmond?" Percy asked his voice betraying his surprise. "What are you doing here?"

"Uncle received the alarm while we were talking over a glass of brandy and invited me along," Edmond replied.

"This is highly irregular, Mr. Holmes," the PM said to Mycroft. "I mean one civilian is concern enough, but two?"

"I can assure you, my lord my nephews are the very soul of discretion. If you have any question, I suggest you take it up with her majesty. She is rather taken with my secretary and partner in the Home Office."

Edmond felt his father's eyes on him. He had yet to

speak with his father regarding his decision. Turning to his uncle, he whispered a warning in his ear. Mycroft nodded once and clarified.

"With his parents' permission and blessing of course."

"Well, I don't like it," the PM harrumphed.

"Give us a moment, my lord," Holmes beckoned him out of the room. The PM protested up until Holmes shut the door on him. "Well," he began when they were alone. "We will discuss this later," Holmes motioned to both Mycroft and Edmond. "But I am pleased. Now since you were so good as to preserve the scene, how about you tell us what you've discover so far," Holmes said.

Mycroft looked to Edmond to explain.

"As you can see, sir, the safe looks forced but on further examination that was a façade to show the initial opening was done by someone with knowledge of the combination," Edmond indicated what he meant.

"A smokescreen?" Percy asked.

"Indeed," Edmond continued.

"It would have to have been someone close to him," Percy said.

"We do have a suspect in custody," Gregson revealed. All the Holmes's turned to look at him. "What?" he grunted.

"Why did you not mention this before?" Holmes asked harshly.

"Well, I...I didn't think it was..." Gregson said.

"Oh come, come who is it, man?" Holmes demanded.

"Well sir, he be the young man who had dinner with Sir Reginald tonight," he explained. "Sir Cedric Somers."

"What?" Percy and Edmond questioned.

"Cedric?" Holmes replied. "No, no, that's not right at all."

"He was the only one—" Gregson started.

"I tell you, Gregson you have the wrong man," Holmes cut him off.

"He's the only other one in the house. Claims he was drugged as well," Gregson said.

"Then he was drugged," Percy replied.

Holmes pulled out a pad of note paper from his pocket

and scribbled a note.

"Have one of your men take this 'round to Dr. Watson's flat. I want him to come and examine Cedric," Holmes ordered.

"Very good, Sir," Gregson agreed and passed it off to a uniform officer by the door.

"Where is he?" Edmond questioned. "I want to see him."

"The accused is in the dining room," Gregson said.

Percy and Edmond walked out of the room and headed to Cedric's side.

"Ced?" Percy called to his friend when he saw him seated at the dining table. Cedric looked up. The usually impeccably dressed Cedric was completely disheveled. His dark hair was askew and his glassy eyes were unfocused.

"Percy? Edmond?" He squinted. "Thank God you've come!"

"What happened, my dear fellow?" Percy asked placing a comforting hand on his friend's shoulder.

"I'm not sure," Cedric replied. "It's all so hazy. All I remember is Hardy, Spooner and I were at cards and we started feeling sluggish and almost drunk but we both had barely two glasses at dinner. Then I woke up to Burns, Hardy's butler, shaking me awake telling me he had sent for the police. Hardy was unresponsive. Thank god the ambulance got here when it did. I was told he was still alive but so heavily drugged they were not sure if he would have survived any longer without medical attention."

Holmes walked over, having stood in the doorway listening to his story.

"Cedric," he called. Cedric's eyes lightened with relief when he saw Holmes.

"Oh, thank Heaven you are here, sir!" He said. "I tried to tell the police all I know but they are determined I'm lying and intentionally drugged Hardy. I don't even know what happened. They're questioning me about a state document. On my father's grave, sir, I know nothing about any such document."

"I believe you, Cedric," Holmes said. His eyes trailed to Gregson who had walked up behind him. "Have you been searched?"

"No, sir, but I have no objection," Cedric replied.

"As much as we believe you, I think the police would be more inclined to believe you if they performed a search." Holmes explained.

"I would be happy to comply if it clears my name," Cedric said. A policeman came up beside Gregson.

"Take him to another room and search him," Gregson ordered.

When Cedric passed Holmes, he stopped and turned to look at him.

"You do believe me, sir?" Cedric asked pleadingly.

Holmes nodded once. Once Cedric was out of the room, Holmes turned to Gregson.

"You did see the state of his eyes, did you not?" Holmes asked.

"Eh? His... his eyes?" Gregson asked. "I can't say that would be something I looked deep into, if you forgive me," Gregson said with a laugh.

"I did, father," Percy stepped forward.

"Probably a powdered opiate or some such drug," Edmond expounded.

"Not something you can fake. You see a faker would never be able to change his eyes," Mycroft answered from behind his brother.

"Precisely," Holmes said. "You have the wrong man, Gregson."

"Hmm, well as long as the search comes back without incident, he will be free to go," Gregson said. "But mark my words, just because he may be without the document doesn't mean he didn't have an accomplice he could have passed it off to in the ensuing confusion."

"That man has been my brother's and my best friend since we were in Primary School, Inspector," Percy stepped forward. "I can assure you, if he swears on his father's grave, then he is innocent."

"Well, as much as you foreigners hold to your gentlemanly words, we English have this little thing called gut instinct," Gregson said. Percy stepped forward almost menacingly at Gregson's obvious slur. Edmond stopped him coming up beside him and placed a hand on his brother's chest.

"*Ne pas le faire*," Edmond told him. Percy's menacing glare at the Inspector was met with a dumb expression of confusion. "*Calme-toi, mon frère*," Edmond soothed. Percy's clenched hand around his swordstick, slowly loosened. Percy looked at Edmond who nodded once, still holding him back.

Percy's gaze went back to Gregson and a sneer marred his handsome features. Breaking from his brother's hold, Percy walked over to the opposite side of the room. A policeman cleared his throat.

"Yes? What is it?" Gregson asked turning, oblivious to the insult he had just dealt and its aftermath. Mycroft stepped around his brother and went to his nephew. Percy's entire body shook with anger.

"Thank you," Holmes whispered to his brother as he passed him. Mycroft nodded once, and Edmond took his place beside his father.

"Forgive me, sir but, a Dr. Watson is here, asking to be admitted," the officer explained.

"Bring him in," Gregson replied.

Holmes walked around the dining room table, which hadn't been cleared.

"What are you looking for, sir?" Edmond asked.

"What do you think?" Holmes asked testing him.

Edmond watched him sniff the food on the plates.

"If you permit me, sir," Edmond started. "I do not believe it would be in the quail."

"Quite so," Holmes answered. He saw Percy shake out of his anger after a low conversation with his uncle and turn back to the room just as Watson walked in.

"Come in, Watson, old chap, how are you?" Holmes asked.

"What on earth, Holmes? I am the last one here I see..." Watson eyed Percy up and down. Alexandra spoke fondly of him after he had left that evening... a little too fondly for a father's liking. "What devilish business are you involved in now."

"Dear old Watson, I needed the best doctor I knew. We

have a patient for you," Holmes said.

"Oh, indeed?" Watson asked. "So, the game is afoot once more?"

"Yes, we would like you to examine a young man and see if his claim of being drugged tonight is a genuine one," Holmes explained.

"Well, lead me to him," Watson said.

Gregson indicated the other room and Watson followed.

"Oh, Gregson," Holmes called him back. "Is Sir Reginald able to speak to us yet?"

"He's still unconscious, Mr. Holmes, he was taken to the hospital. It appears he got more of the drug than Sir Cedric," Gregson explained.

"I will need to speak with him," Holmes said.

Gregson left the room with Dr. Watson. Holmes, Percy, Edmond and Mycroft were alone.

"Quickly," Holmes said and indicated the decanter of wine on the table. "Percy, hand me the bowl. Edmond, come here, you have the steadiest hands. Pour as much of the wine as you can into this container." Holmes showed him a vial.

Both men did as their father asked. Holmes held the bowl Percy had handed him under the vial into which Edmond poured the wine.

"You think it's in the wine?" Percy asked watching his brother pour.

"Undoubtedly," Holmes answered. "Look at their plates; none of the items are pungent enough to conceal the taste of whatever it was. Look at the other place setting," Holmes indicated the third place. "He had no wine."

"What sort of drug do you think it is?" Edmond asked, watching his pouring with absolute fervor.

"Some sort of barbiturate probably," Holmes said. "I won't know until I test it."

"Done," Edmond said as he finished.

"Excellent," Holmes replied. "Set it back to its precise location. Everything must have the appearance of being untouched."

Once settled, Holmes turned to Percy who hadn't

moved from his position staring at the places.

"What is it, son?" He asked.

Percy said nothing, but his eyes scanned the table.

"Percy?" Holmes went over to him. Almost with a start, Percy jerked out of his stupor.

"Forgive me, Sir," he said. "I was just thinking."

"Good, what about this time?" Holmes asked.

"Well, as you know I had a dinner engagement this evening which I cancelled last minute," Percy started.

"Yes, so you could spend the evening with Miss Watson and your sister," Holmes said.

"Indeed, I'll not deny it. But you see, this table is laid for four people," Percy continued.

"One of which was meant for you," Holmes surmised.

"Indeed, I was to meet Cedric at his flat and we were to ride together," Percy explained.

"Perfectly sound," Holmes said.

"The thing that bothers me, is there are four places, yet only three people. I knew of no other fourth person. My place is clear by the lack of a place setting," he indicated the extra chair. "They must have realized I would not be joining them. Cedric's and Sir Reginald's places both have food and drink on them, but then so does the fourth place as you mentioned."

"You are wondering who this fourth man is and where he is? You wonder if he has anything to do with this?" Holmes offered.

"I am, sir," Percy replied.

"Perfectly sound logic," Holmes answered. "Either this man drugged the others to steal the document Sir Reginald had in his safe, or he woke out of his stupor before the others and seeing what happened, did not want to be a part of a scandal. Seeing no wine at his place, I believe it is obvious which answer is correct. Your observations are remarkable. Let's see if the police and the good doctor are finished with Cedric and see if we can speak with him about this illusive man at dinner."

Chapter Ten

A man hurried through the darkened streets of Whitechapel. He passed pub after pub. Twice, he was approached by women outside a brothel, but he kept walking. Pulling his cloak around him, he felt the papers in his hand burn like a roaring fire.

He ignored yet another woman and walked on. He had no time to change his clothes and even though they screamed wealth, he was worried someone would recognize him in the card houses and brothels he frequented. Worried the men he was eluding, until he had the money to pay them, would find him, he drew his coat collar up to shield his face. Hunching against the wind, he saw the cab he was looking for a few feet ahead.

He knocked on the door five times in sequence of two, pause, two, pause, and one. The door swung open and he stepped in.

"Did you get it?" The man, sitting in the shadows, asked.

"Yes," he answered.

"Any problems?" The man asked.

"None, luckily Charles Holmes was not at the dinner. It would have been difficult to deceive him," he answered.

"Let me deal with the Holmes's," the man said. "Give me the document."

"Sir, it's not that I do not trust you. A man of your reputation is of course above suspicion, but might I have the money you promised me, first?" he asked.

"Well done," the other man laughed. "It's refreshing to have someone challenge me. Here you are, Spooner, here's your ten thousand pounds," the man handed him a case.

"Thank you, Sir," Spooner revealed the documents from under his cloak and handed them to him.

"Oh, one more thing," the man in the darkness said. Spooner looked back at him. "You must never reveal my identity."

"I swear to you, sir, I will be as silent as the grave," Spooner said.

"Oh, I'm certain of it," the man replied.

There was a ruckus in the room across the way and as the Holmes men rushed in, they found Watson fuming, staring at Cedric whose hands were raised in supplication.

"I assure you, Doctor," Cedric was saying. "I did not do what it is you are accusing me of doing. I did not do more than what you saw. I swear it to you. Your daughter is still an innocent."

"Not as much of one as before you came into her life, you rogue!" Watson cried.

"Doctor, I swear to you," Cedric started. "Alexandra is-"

"Miss Watson to you, you fiend," Watson exclaimed.

"Miss Watson is a charming young woman and I very much care for her, but it is not what you assume. Percy, tell him, I would never take advantage of a young woman."

Percy's eyes darted back and forth between Cedric and Watson.

"I take it you know Miss Watson then?" Percy's voice was tight.

"Aye he knows her," Watson replied. "He stole her first kiss."

"I did not steal anything, she bestowed it upon me," Cedric said. Percy turned on his heels and walked out of the room. Mycroft gave a low whistle and shook his head.

"Oh, for god's sake," Sherlock cried. "Will I never have peace from this drama? Watson, it is clear the boy did nothing untoward, now could you, for the love of god, do what it is I called you to do?"

"No, this fiend—" Watson started.

"Watson," Holmes barked in a tone Edmond had heard him use when either he or Percy were in trouble for speaking to him in a manner he did not appreciate. From the looks of it, Watson had the same reaction they had whenever they heard that voice. He snapped his eyes to Holmes, paled slightly but eventually nodded.

He turned back to Cedric and eyed him.

"You swear on all you hold dear, you did not compromise my daughter," Watson said.

"I swear to you, Sir," Cedric replied. "I cared deeply for Alexandra. Had certain issues in my personal life not made it impossible for me to marry, I would have gladly become her husband. But that was not to be. What you saw was a goodbye, nothing more. Miss Watson is a lovely young woman and any man would be fortunate to have her as a wife," Cedric said. "It is just not my fortune to have her as mine."

Watson eventually nodded and turned back to Holmes.

"Done?" Holmes asked sarcastically.

"How would you feel, Holmes if it were Rebecca?" Watson asked.

"Privileged my daughter choose wisely," Holmes stated. Cedric stared at him. "Now shall we begin? Cedric, go and find Percy and explain the situation. Dear lord that is all I need, two Frenchmen dueling over a woman." Cedric looked at him confused but nodded. Edmond followed explaining why Percy reacted the way he did.

"Any sign of the document, Gregson?" Holmes asked.

"None, Mr. Holmes," he replied.

"And, Watson will you confirm if Cedric was drugged?"

Holmes asked.

"Yes, according to what I saw, he was," Watson replied.

"Thank you," Holmes answered. "So, is he free to go, Gregson?"

"Yes, Mr. Holmes he can go," Gregson said.

"Very decent of you," Holmes' tone was dripping with condescension to only those ears who knew him the best. Gregson and the policeman behind him left the room. Cedric, Percy and Edmond reentered the room. Edmond caught his father's gaze and rolled his eyes. Holmes laughed at his son's reaction. Edmond hated drama as much as he did.

"I've never been so humiliated in my life," Cedric said as he straightened his waistcoat and neck tie.

"Oh, come now, old man," Holmes said. "It is clear you are not a suspect. It was merely to prove Gregson wrong."

"Not for the search, Mr. Holmes although if it weren't for you I would probably be facing a firing squad right now... Honestly, to arrest a man solely on the accent of his voice should be illegal... Frog indeed. If he only knew who my father was — and simply because I do not speak English with that absurd accent of his, I am suspect," Cedric replied. His French accent becoming more pronounced.

"Now, now, we must allow we are in a foreign land and even though both our fathers are British, it is where we grew up that is questioned," Edmond said. "It is all over now."

"Thankfully, yes," he answered. "Thank you for believing me," he looked at each one individually and his eyes rested longer on Percy than all the others.

"My dear fellow, after having known you practically your whole life, as if I would allow it," Holmes said.

"I thank you, sir," Cedric replied bowing stiffly.

"Why don't you come home with us? We could do with a strong drink," Percy offered.

"Thank you, I would enjoy that," Cedric said.

"By the way, whatever happened to the third man at dinner?" Holmes asked before they left.

"Third man?" Cedric asked. "Oh, you mean, Spooner."

"Spooner?" Holmes prompted.

"Harry—Henry Spooner... isn't he here?" Cedric asked.

"It doesn't appear so," Mycroft said.

"Well, the last thing I remember we were all seated at cards. He may have awakened before the rest of us," Cedric offered.

"Do you know where he lives?" Holmes said.

"Honestly, I have only known him some little time."

"Ah well, when Hardy wakes we must ask him," Percy said.

"Oh, Percy, don't you know where he lives?" Holmes asked.

"Me, sir?" Percy asked surprised. "No, I can't say I do."

"Hmm, pity. Edmond?" Holmes asked.

"Somewhere in St. George's Square I would say, sir," Edmond replied.

"Quite so," Holmes answered.

"How on earth do you know that?" Watson asked.

"Well," Holmes started and indicated Edmond to explain.

"There was a good deal of mud in the entryway. Having ruled out the tracks made by the policemen, our tracks..." he indicated his uncle and himself, "...are distinctly from Pall Mall as one would expect due to the coloration of the earth. Yours," he indicated Percy and Cedric, "are from Kensington where you are staying with Cedric for the time. The consistency is obvious. Father has no mud on his boots from getting into a cab on cobblestone and getting out of the cab here on brick. That left a very distinct mud pattern from St. George's Square."

"Really, Edmond, you astonish me," Holmes stated. Edmond just shrugged. "Now, let us get back to Baker Street so I can figure out what drug was used in the wine," Holmes said.

"Mr. Holmes," a voice called before they left. All six men turned towards the Prime Minister. "Are you any closer to discovering where the document is?"

"I do indeed, my lord," Holmes said.

"Have you no hope of getting it back?" He begged.

"I have," Holmes said. "But it may take time."

"But that is time we do not have," he pleaded.

"My lord, you have been good enough to come to me for one or two little problems in the past. May I ask your faith in me be based on those previous successes? I have not let you or England down before and I certainly do not intend to let either of you down now. Good morning, my lord," Holmes walked out of the house and hailed a cab.

Chapter Eleven

Marguerite heard her husband's step on the stair. Closing the novel she read by the light of a candle, she got up and reached for her housecoat. Tying it around her, she opened the door to see all six men filing into the study. She quickly closed the door before anyone but her husband saw her. She heard Sherlock excuse himself from the group.

"Margot," he whispered. She emerged from behind the dressing screen in a light blue morning dress. Her hair lay loose about her shoulders.

"Is everything all right, Sherlock?" She asked going over to him.

"Complicated, my dear," he answered.

"Could you..." she turned to expose the back of her dress, unbuttoned. Holmes attempted to button her dress, as she went on. "Should I have breakfast prepared?"

"No, my love, that would not be necessary," he replied focusing on a button hole causing him difficulties. "Perhaps some coffee or tea though?"

She moved her hair so he could button the top.

"Of course," she answered. When he finished, he leaned down to kiss her shoulder just above the fabric of the dress. She made a small sound that was between a hum and a sigh. "Was that Cedric I saw?" She asked turning in to him and wrapping her arms around him. He pushed a stray piece of hair behind her ear.

"It was, he was a witness to the crime. The poor man had been drugged. He's all right now, though," he clarified seeing her worry. "I also have a confession, it appears Cedric and Alexandra have been acquainted and he was nearly attacked tonight by Watson. Apparently, Cedric was the first man to kiss her."

"Oh, my love that is old news," she replied removing a speck off his jacket.

"You knew," he stated, not surprised. He had not spent enough time with Alexandra to notice her reactions.

"My darling, a woman knows what it feels like to speak of the man she cares for. When I mentioned Cedric to Alexandra earlier, a blush grew on her cheek. I, of course, knew then, there was something between them. Of course, our Cedric is too much of a gentleman to have taken it further, but it is the same look I had after our first rendezvous in the garden of my father's house, if you recall." She straightened his collar.

"Hmm," Holmes answered. "It seems I have underestimated your knowledge of young women, my love."

"You forget I used to be one," she replied.

"I have not forgotten," he answered. "You are just as beautiful, nay more so now than you were then and I am privileged to have been your first kiss and first in all things."

"Are you testing *my* blushing ability, Sherlock?" she teased.

"It is for a case, my darling," he teased.

She laughed melodiously. "What case is this?" she asked stepping away from him to her dressing table. Sitting at the bench, she began brushing her hair.

Holmes explained what had happened earlier that evening and as he heard the clock tower chime five times the top of the hour, he amended from that *evening* to that *morning*.

"I have a feeling this will not be the last we will hear of

a missing document."

Marguerite began pinning her impressive amount of chocolate colored hair.

"How interesting," she said looking at him in the mirror.

"Very," he replied. "But rather open and shut. We only have to wait for the documents to appear."

"It sounds as if you are not convinced they have left England's shores."

"I don't," he answered.

"Well, let us hope for a peaceful ending to this horrid business," she said standing. "Still, it is good to see you return." When Holmes said nothing, she continued. "You are an absolute bear when you have not had a case, even with us as a distraction to you," she stated patting his cheek. "Welcome back," she whispered before she kissed him quickly and stepped out the door to welcome her guests.

Holmes smiled slightly at her touch and words. Yes, he knew he had been a bear to his family the other day combing the newspaper for something... not boring. But, Marguerite knew him far too well. Sighing, he went to the wash basin in their room and splashed some water on his face. Taking off his coat, he loosened his collar and rolled up his shirt sleeves. Drying the water off his face and arms, he went to his wardrobe and searched for the chemicals he would need.

Chapter Twelve

"Edmond," Holmes called from his position next to his chemical lab. Edmond looked over from the window, his father beckoned to him to come over. "I need your steady hands. This is the second to the last test I can perform. We only have enough wine for two more."

"I understand, Sir," Edmond said, taking the vial of wine.

"Just a little bit," Holmes stressed.

Edmond focused and poured just enough into the concoction Holmes had created. They waited.

"Confound it!" Holmes said as he crossed out a name on his note pad and sighed. He went to the fireplace, took a cigarette from his case, lit it and paced in front of the fire. "I've tried everything," Holmes said indignantly. "I only have enough for one more test and I have two options."

"What about a Chinese drug?" Percy offered.

"I've tried three," Holmes stated. Everyone waited. Eventually, he turned back and pinned Cedric with a stare. "Cedric, when you woke do you recall anything? A faint smell, a disgusting taste in your mouth? Anything at all?"

"No, sir," Cedric shook his head.

"If I have nothing to work with how am I expected to work?" Holmes demanded and continued to pace. Watson handed Cedric a whisky soda. Cedric looked up at him surprised.

"Don't worry, he gets like this, it's nothing to do with you," Watson said. "I find this helps," he indicated the whisky. Cedric thanked him and accepted the drink. Watson sat beside him on the chaise lounge. "I also wanted to tell you, though I do not apologize, I was wrong. I was merely acting as a father and what I saw, startled me. It made me see my little girl as a woman and that is not something a father ever wants to see. So, I ask you to forgive my overreaction. Holmes would say I do that far too often."

"Thank you, Sir, and to be honest I acted like a cad," he admitted. "I should never have… acted thusly in your home or in any circle unless we were properly engaged. For that, I am truly sorry. But I promise you, I have the utmost respect for you and your daughter. I did desire her as a wife, but it was not to be," his eyes drifted to Percy. "I only ask you to consider there may be others who are interested in her and also have the greatest respect."

Watson nodded once but still had his reservations. His eyes followed Cedric's to Percy lounging in his father's armchair. After a moment, Cedric yawned.

"Are you still feeling its affects?" Watson asked snapping out of his thoughts. Cedric nodded. "How about you rest?" Watson went on. Holmes cursed loudly. "If you can, with all this noise," he amended.

"Watson!" Holmes stopped dead in his tracks and stared at him. "You are brilliant! You are absolutely brilliant!" he exclaimed.

"Yes, yes I'm not luminous myself but I am a conductor of light, I know. Go on, what did I say that made the way illuminated?" Watson asked sarcastically.

"Cedric, you have no issue I'm sure, with needles?" Holmes asked.

"Umm… no, sir," he answered.

"Excellent," Holmes went back to his chemicals. Watson stood and went over to his friend. "I've been following a wonderful bit of scientific discovery stemming from the day we met, Watson, when I found the reagent that reacts to hemoglobin."

"I recall," Watson answered. "But that was merely to test which stains could be blood."

"At first, yes," Holmes went on. "But with that knowledge, I continued my research and found a way to treat an infected person's blood to see what foreign agents may be present." He held out instruments to Watson. "One vial of his blood is all I need, Watson," Holmes said.

Cedric looked up, his eyes slightly nervous. Edmond sat beside him.

"I've never had this done," he said.

"There is nothing to worry about," Edmond replied. Cedric looked over at him. "I've done this multiple times, as has Percy. I believe we were reading the same article, Father." Holmes said nothing while he worked. "It's actually rather interesting, you see, blood is a very intriguing—"

"Ow," Cedric said and looked over at Watson.

"All done," Watson replied.

Cedric looked back at Edmond, "thank you," he said.

"No trouble at all," Edmond replied.

Holmes took the vial from Watson and began to work.

Four hours later, Cedric had fallen asleep on the chaise lounge, Percy dozed in the arm chair, Watson sat across from him reading the newspaper, and Edmond stood by the window looking out to the streets, one foot resting on the small ledge a few inches above the floor.

"I've found it!" Holmes cried, jerking his son and Cedric awake. Edmond looked over unfazed.

"What is it?" Watson asked.

"Edmond was right," he said. "It's a derivative of opium, one I have only seen once before. It really is most remarkable. I have not had the pleasure of seeing this specific—"

A knock at the study door interrupted him. Mrs. Hudson and Marguerite came in.

"I hope he hasn't kept you up all morning," Marguerite said helping Mrs. Hudson set the tray down.

"Margot, we are right in the middle of an experiment, this is no time to eat," Holmes complained.

She looked over at him. "You forget, my love, you are the only one in this room who feels that way."

"Margot, this is the breakthrough we have been waiting for, do you expect we can be delayed even for a moment?" He asked.

She put her hands on her hips and stared at her husband, an eyebrow raised.

"Do you expect me to allow our sons, Cedric, Mycroft and dear Dr. Watson to go a full twelve hours without food after having to endure your experiments?" She asked.

"Marguerite, don't you realize—" he paused when he saw the look in her eyes.

"You know me better than that, Sherlock," she said.

"You are right, forgive me. I was not thinking," he replied.

"Oh, you were thinking, just not of food," she answered. "Eat, please," she said gesturing to the food laid out before them.

Rebecca woke at her usual time that morning. As she dressed, she heard voices downstairs. Walking down to the closed study door, she opened it without knocking and immediately regretted it.

"Oh, forgive me," she said seeing the men at breakfast. They all stood when she entered. Her eyes lighted upon Cedric. "Cedric," her smile lit the room.

"It's good to see you again, Rebecca," he replied.

A part of her wanted to run to him, but she remembered her place, stepped forward and extended her hand. He took it and kissed it gently. Feeling the lightning that raced through her hand as they touched caused her to clear her throat and look away.

"Forgive me for interrupting your breakfast. Dr. Watson, Uncle it is very good to see you."

"My goodness, my dear," her uncle said. "Every man between fifteen and fifty will want to dance with you this season. You are a truly beautiful young woman, the image of your mother."

She blushed slightly. Cedric visibly bristled at the idea.

"I thank you," she said in a small voice.

"Come, my dear, we can make room for you," Holmes said. "Are you hungry at all?"

"Please, do not worry, Papa," she answered. "I will be very happy to take a plate to my room."

"Nonsense," Edmond stated.

Cedric indicated his place. "Please, I am finished. Take my seat," he offered.

"Thank you," she replied.

"Your mother just stepped out for a moment, my dear. We were discussing a very interesting little problem we've been presented," Holmes explained.

"One of your fascinating little cases that dear Dr. Watson has been so wonderful as to make famous?" She asked. Watson chuckled.

"A pretty puzzle," Mycroft replied.

Cedric stepped around to the mantle. "One I'm afraid I am right in the middle of," Cedric said pulling out his cigarette case. "Do you mind if I smoke?" He asked indicating his case. She shook her head. He struck a match and lifted it to the tobacco.

"A state document of vast importance has been stolen," Percy explained.

"Any hope in retrieving it?" She asked.

"Very little." Holmes explained what happened the previous evening and into the early morning hours. Rebecca turned a worry-filled face to the twenty-five-year-old man by the mantle. He raised his hand slightly indicating he was perfectly all right.

"You, no doubt, do not expect to find this Mr. Spooner alive," she said.

"What do you mean, my dear?" Holmes asked.

"Only that wouldn't it be possible he is already dead?" She asked.

"Give us your theory, Rebecca," her uncle replied.

"Well, I ... I don't mean to—"

"Go on," Edmond coaxed.

"This Mr. Spooner, you have said, appeared disheveled, Cedric," she said. He nodded. "Well couldn't that be an indication he either got ready in a hurry or he had no manservant to help him? A man, confident enough to have dinner with two high ranking men of society, would clearly not be poor unless he is rich in name only. But as you said, he has no title or rank.

"Following this line of reasoning, he must then come from money. Would it not be then, he would have a manservant? Unless of course, he has fallen upon hard times? There has been no massive fluctuation in the London Stock Exchange recently, or that would have been far more important news than the family of Sherlock Holmes. Therefore, his considerable losses must have been of his own making. Perhaps he visited the rather unsavory parts of town and gotten himself into debt.

"He would then be of easy access to someone willing to give him money or overlook his debts if he got them something in return. They must know he is good friends with a Foreign Office Official, perhaps he mentioned it while inebriated. They heard of this document so, they ask him to get it, promising great reward, but when he does get it, he knows who they are. They cannot allow him to live so they dispose of him and take this document out of the country. They have what they wanted and did not have to pay any money for it. It seems the easiest way. And though I have no knowledge of those rather unsavory places, I have a good indication of what goes on there from the stories of others."

Everyone had fallen silent as she spoke. Holmes had a smirk on his face. Percy held a spoon halfway to his mouth staring at her. Cedric held his cigarette between his fingers, frozen, watching her.

Her eyes darted from one to the other of them, and

then looked down.

"That is only my theory," she said.

Holmes began to chuckle. "Just like your mother," he said with a sparkle in his eye. Marguerite came into the room having listened to her daughter from the doorway.

"A perfectly sound theory, *ma Cherie*," Marguerite said. "And perhaps the correct one. Sherlock, Inspector Gregson is downstairs. He said it is most urgent you go with him."

Holmes nodded and stood.

"Coming?" He looked at Watson, Percy and Edmond as he pulled on his coat.

"Oh yes," they all shook themselves from their surprise.

"You go on, Sherlock, this whole confounded business has made me dash tired. I shall return to the Diogenes. Send for me if you need help." Mycroft said.

Holmes, Watson, Percy and Edmond filed past Marguerite and Rebecca.

"Coming, Cedric?" Holmes popped his head back into the room. Cedric agreed and threw his cigarette into the fire, nodding to the two ladies on his way out.

Chapter Thirteen

"It's murder, Mr. Holmes, as clear as anything," Gregson said to Holmes, Watson and Percy as they bounced around the streets of London in a police cab. Edmond and Cedric had hailed a cab after them and rode behind.

"Well, don't let's talk about it yet, Gregson; let's wait until we're all together," Holmes said.

"Might I ask one question, sir?" Percy asked his father. Holmes nodded. "The murdered person, is it a man or woman?"

"A man, dressed like a toff, evening clothes, there was no identification on the body," Gregson said. "He was shot—"

"Please, Gregson, I hate having things repeated. Let us wait for the others before mentioning anything else in regard to the case," Holmes said.

They passed some of the way in silence. It wasn't until ten minutes later, Percy turned to Gregson.

"Is there any particular reason you are staring at me in that all-too-intrusive way, Inspector?" He asked.

"Oh, I – uh – I'm sorry, Mr. Holmes," he stuttered.

"Is there something you need?" Percy asked.

"I was just captured by how similar you look to Mr. Holmes, here, apart from your dark blonde hair; you both could pass as identical."

"So you believe he is my son, now?" Holmes demanded.

"The missus thrust a newspaper in my face when I came home and told her. She claims to have followed your story in the paper. How old you are?" Gregson asked.

"I am twenty-four years old," he answered.

"And your brother?" He asked.

"Edmond is just twenty-three," Percy replied.

"Very close in age then," Gregson surmised.

"It would appear so," Percy replied condescendingly.

"They are eleven months apart," Holmes explained.

"Blyme, Mr. Holmes you were busy," he slapped his knee laughing. "But then I can understand why, your wife is —"

He stopped himself when he saw the look in both Percy's and Holmes' faces.

"Sorry," he said.

"Is there anything else?" Percy asked seeing him still looking at him after a few moments.

"Sorry, I didn't realize I'm staring. It was too impossible to believe. Now, I'm in a cab with Mr. Holmes and have met his sons... it's so real. It's hard for me to comprehend," Gregson explained.

"That's how I felt, Gregson, but in my case, it was switched. I met them first and then read about it," Watson said.

"I would like to hear that story," Gregson said.

The cab came to a stop.

"I'm afraid that story will have to wait. It appears we have reached our destination," Holmes said opening the cab door and getting out. He saw Edmond's and Cedric's cab pull up behind theirs and they stepped out.

Edmond walked over to his father. "What have you learned?"

"I asked Gregson to wait until we were all together," Holmes explained.

They turned towards the beach. The police stood guard over a tarp covered figure on the ground.

"Mr. Holmes," Cedric said. Holmes turned to him. "May I ask why you want me here?"

"If this is Spooner, only you among us could identify him. A quick identification will help me on my investigation," Holmes explained.

"Is that the only reason?" He asked.

"Oh, you mean do I want to interrogate you about your intentions towards my daughter? Possibly, but since there is a dead body and you both have had a difficult time hiding your growing fondness for each other since she was old enough to understand what it was, that can wait. Besides you know if your intentions towards her are admirable, we will not have a problem. If they are not, well... let's not find out what I'll do, shall we?" Holmes smiled at him quickly and walked away.

Cedric blinked. "That was not what I meant at all. I had merely thought due to the recent history between myself and the police, is it proper for me to be here?" He felt the heat rise to his face and Watson looked over at him.

"Yes, he's always like that," Watson said. "And I am sure it will be fine."

"All right, men, we'll take it from here," Gregson said to the policemen guarding the body. They saluted and walked away.

"I know I don't need to tell you to prepare yourself, Mr. Holmes, but all the same, it is rather gruesome," Gregson warned.

He pulled back the tarp to reveal the body of a young man. A bullet wound between his eyes was the apparent cause of death but there was a symbol carved around the bullet wound in his forehead. Cedric's stomach twisted and he turned away from the body covering his mouth.

"The fiend," Watson breathed.

Edmond crouched down opposite his father to take a closer look, unfazed by the depravity of the killing.

"Death was instantaneous," Edmond observed.

"Close range, too," Holmes replied. "See the powder burns around the wound?"

"Twenty-two? Or something a little bigger?" Edmond asked.

"Twenty-two sounds about right," Holmes answered.

Cedric walked back and stood beside Percy.

"Spooner?" Holmes asked looking up at him.

Cedric nodded. "Poor devil," he said. Edmond stood up beside his friend. "What's that symbol engraved into his forehead?

"It's a Yin Yang," Edmond replied. "It represents light and dark. It's the Chinese symbol for balance in the world."

"China, eh?" Gregson asked. "So, it is them Boxers."

"I doubt it," Holmes answered.

"See how they used the powder burns as the dark and left the light side alone?" Edmond indicated.

Cedric, Gregson, and Watson stared at him blankly.

"Edmond, for those who don't know," Holmes said. "Why don't you show them?"

Edmond looked at his father and then his brother. He started unbuttoning his shirt. Gregson and Watson stared at him. Edmond pulled his shirt to one side. They gathered around and looked at the tattoo he was showing on the left side of his chest over his heart. It was a circle divided in two by a wavy line but the same on both sides, one side darker with a white dot in the larger bulbous portion and the other side white with a black dot at the opposite end. Edmond released his shirt and began re-buttoning.

"China for eight years," he explained when they looked at him.

"What were you doing there for that long?" Watson asked.

"Studying," Edmond replied.

"Studying? Studying what?" Gregson asked.

Edmond looked at Holmes and motioned his head towards the pier. Edmond pulled off his jacket and handed it to his brother then slipped out of his shoes. They faced the pier and Edmond bounced a little, loosening his limbs.

He ran as fast as he could and scaled the fifteen-foot pier. When he reached the top of it, he flipped backwards off the pier and landed on his feet facing his father a few yards off. He raced to him. They threw punches and Edmond kicked lowering half of his body so low to the ground on multiple occasions, his kicks were near Holmes' face. Their routine was almost a blur but they never actually hit each other. Their accuracy, well practiced. Edmond flipped backwards from Holmes three times using his hands twice and then not touching the ground on the last one. Holmes took a stance, lowered his hands like a stirrup, and nodded. Edmond nodded once and took off running toward Holmes. Watson's eyes grew big as he saw Edmond leap into the air step into his father's hand and Holmes carried the momentum pushing him higher into the air. Edmond flipped midair and landed on his feet, two yards away, his legs bent and his arms in a formation unfamiliar to the rest of them.

After a moment, Edmond turned back to Holmes and they both bowed to each other. Barely panting, he walked over to Percy who helped him back into his coat.

"Show off," Percy winked.

Edmond laughed. "Studying the martial arts," Edmond explained.

"Well," Watson blinked when he heard Holmes' voice as he walked up. "That was invigorating," Holmes said. "We haven't done that recently."

"You didn't even blink, Mr. Holmes. How did you know he would clear it?" Gregson asked.

"Because he has yet to not," Holmes said. "Now then, I think anything related to the Orient should be Edmond's territory."

"Can you tell if this man's killer is one of them Boxers?" Gregson asked.

Edmond looked at the body for a moment. Then shook his head.

"No, he was not," he answered.

"How can you tell?" Cedric asked.

"Well, after spending eight years over there I know their ways. They would not kill with a bullet, too noisy. They prefer a quieter method. That coupled with the fact the documents in question are in his inner breast pocket somewhat indicates this man was not in the Boxers' employ." Edmond explained.

He crouched down and moved Spooner's lapel with a

pen so they could see what he saw.

"Lord love a duck," Gregson exclaimed grabbing the paper from the pocket. "It's all here. It is exactly ten pages just like the Prime Minister said it would be. Wonderful!"

"Now that mystery is solved, it's time to turn our attention to who murdered this man," Holmes said.

"Father," Percy called. "I seem to recall a case not six months ago, before we came over to London, you told us about. One about Oriental men being found murdered on the steps of MPs homes. It was just after you left for London on your last visit to France before we joined you. Do you recall the case?"

"I do," Holmes replied. "Three men between the ages of nineteen and thirty-two found dead. No obvious causes of death. Do you still have the case notes, Watson?"

"On my desk, I was just working on writing that case up this week in fact," Watson said.

"Try not to be so lurid in your descriptions, Watson," Holmes replied.

"I will report it like I always do," he answered.

"With pomp and circumstance?" Holmes replied.

"If you're implying I inflate the truth about these cases of ours, you are sadly mistake—"

"Gentlemen," Percy called. "Please, this is no time to be discussing your personal beliefs on the subject. Father, didn't you say you always suspected it was someone who fought against the Boxers due to what they had tattooed on their hands?"

"The Chinese symbol for death, yes I remember," Holmes said.

"Could this be a copycat?" Percy asked.

"We found the man responsible. He was pronounced insane and released to a psychiatric facility. He was a former British soldier who fought over in China and lost his right hand." Holmes explained.

"The man is behind bars, there is no possible way this could be related to that case at all," Gregson said.

"There's always a chance of it being a copycat, Inspector," Percy replied.

"In any case, gentlemen," Cedric piped up. "I didn't

know Mr. Spooner well, but don't you think he deserves the respect of being transported to the morgue? Someone should tell his fiancée."

"His fiancée?" Holmes asked. "Do you know her name?"

"Yes, a Miss Amelia Austen," he said. "I don't know her myself, but I do remember him speaking of her."

"I better go to the Diogenes and give Uncle these papers," Edmond said.

"I'll come with you," Percy replied. "Though I enjoy speaking to the fair sex I would rather not deliver bad news. A woman crying is not the most irritating thing in the world but it comes close."

"Glad to know you are the compassionate sort," Watson replied.

Percy blanched. "I did not mean to imply..." he cleared his throat. "Of course, my own family, my mother and sister and of course any wife I would be fortunate to have would not be irritating. I merely meant I do not know how to assist them when they are hysterical not that they would be – I simply mean..."

"Percy, come with me," Edmond said stopping him from making an even bigger fool of himself. Edmond headed off to the extra cab in which he had arrived. Percy followed, after apologizing to Watson again.

"Will you accompany me, Mr. Holmes?" Gregson asked.

"I think not, Gregson," Holmes answered. "I am sure you have it all under control. Dr. Watson and I will stay here for the time being. There are one or two minor points I want to clear up before we leave. But Cedric please go if you wish."

"I would rather stay with you, Mr. Holmes," he said. "I do not know the lady in question and I only met Spooner once or twice."

"Very well then," Holmes agreed. "You have everything you need, Gregson?"

"I believe so, sir," he answered.

"Good, come along then, I could use you both," Holmes said.

Chapter

Fourteen

Percy and Edmond walked through the Diogenes Club soundlessly. They headed to their uncle's rooms to give him the information.

Pausing just a moment by door, Edmond took a deep breath. Percy looked over at him.

"*Ça va bien*?" He asked him.

They both heard voices coming from behind the door. Edmond held out the document to Percy.

"You give it to the Prime Minister," he said.

"No," Percy replied. "You found them, Ed. The honor is yours."

"I really want no credit, Percy, besides we are brothers we share in the honor. You know I want nothing to do with this. It is your desire to become a part of politics, not mine. Please, allow me to give you the honor." Edmond said.

Percy observed him closely. Having grown up not even a year apart and without the ability to trust anyone with their identity, Percy counted his brother as his confidante, best friend, and companion. Cedric was the only person they trusted and afterwards The Three Musketeers – as they called each other – were inseparable.

Finally, Percy nodded and accepted the papers.

"If you're sure," Percy said.

"*Absolument*," Edmond replied.

"*Merci*," Percy clapped his brother on the shoulder.

Opening the door to see their uncle and the Prime Minister sitting together before a fire, Percy puffed himself up and took a step forward.

Saying nothing as they walked, Watson and Cedric followed Holmes dutifully through the streets of Whitechapel. Holmes' pace was fast, then he would slow for a moment looking at his feet then his speed would increase. During one of the times Holmes slowed looking around, Watson eyed Cedric.

"How long have you known Holmes?" Watson asked.

"I knew Percy and Edmond at Primary School where they were known as *Maison*; their alias while in hiding," Cedric replied.

"Hiding?" Watson asked. "I knew they were kept there because Holmes wanted them safe, but hiding?"

"Uh-well," Cedric stuttered. "Because of their relationship to—"

"Cedric," Holmes called to him interrupting him. There was a look in Holmes' eyes that stopped Cedric from saying anything more. "Watson, did you notice anything unusual about the crime scene."

"Unusual?" Watson asked. "No, no, I don't think so."

"Hmm, you, Cedric?" Holmes asked.

"No, Sir, I can't say I did," he replied. "Was there something unusual?"

"Think," Holmes said. They both thought for a moment then shrugged. "Watson, do you remember the case back in eighty-eight, the one you luridly titled *The Second Stain*?"

"Uh, yes I believe so. Blackmailer killed by his hot-blooded wife," Watson summarized.

"Yes, good, and do you remember why you named it

that ridiculous name?" Holmes asked.

Watson bit back his response, but then the idea dawned on him.

"You mean, when... *the lady* moved the rug and — lack of blood, that's what was strange, the lack of blood from the head wound," Watson said excitedly when he figured out what Holmes was saying.

"Well done, Watson! I'm glad to see not all my instructions have been for naught," Holmes replied. "Correct me if I am wrong, Doctor, but a wound like that would have bled profusely."

"Well, yes," Watson said.

"So, the lack of blood would indicate?" Holmes coaxed.

"He was killed elsewhere and his body dumped on the shore," Cedric said.

"Precisely," Holmes answered.

"So, you are now looking for the place where he was killed," Watson replied.

"What would a well-dressed man be doing in the alleyways of London?" Holmes asked. "He would definitely draw attention to himself. So... let's find someone who saw him. Detective work is ninety-nine percent leg work, gentlemen. Time to walk."

"It was so very good to see Cedric this morning," Marguerite said as she sipped her tea sitting with her daughter and Alexandra.

Alexandra's eyes sped to Marguerite's.

"Cedric was here?" she asked.

Rebecca looked over at her confused.

"You know him?" She asked.

Alexandra looked down.

"I must confess I do," she answered.

"May I ask...?" Rebecca started. "What was the nature of your relationship?"

A blush rose on Alexandra's cheeks.

"We were courting for a few weeks," she said looking

over at the two ladies. Catching Marguerite's expression, she immediately continued. "But we were always just friends. He is a very wonderful man. I felt privileged to know him."

"Tell us, Alexandra, are you spoken for now?" Marguerite asked.

"No," she replied. "I always thought I would be married by now but honestly, I am not concerned. I have a wonderful father who loves me dearly. Though, of course, a young lady always thinks of a husband and a family."

"What do you think of Percy?" Rebecca asked.

"Well, of course," she replied. "Your brother is very handsome," she stated. "Tell me, Rebecca is there a young man you fancy?"

Rebecca looked over at her mother who winked at her.

"Yes, actually, even though I am not officially *out*," Rebecca started.

"Permit me a guess?" Alexandra's eyes sparkled. Rebecca nodded. "Is he tall?" Rebecca nodded again. "Dark haired?" Rebecca bit her lower lip. "The deepest blue eyes that rival the water?" Rebecca grinned and nodded. "Does he, by chance, have a very elegant accent?" Rebecca's face flushed and she looked away. "I must tell you, Rebecca, Cedric is quite the catch."

The women giggled.

"May I ask a personal question?" Rebecca asked. "And perhaps it's an impertinent one."

"Yes, though it only happened once, I can tell you, he is a man whose kiss is quite enjoyable and desirable," Alexandra winked.

Squealing with laughter, the women toasted each other as Marguerite pulled out a bottle of wine.

Chapter Fifteen

"Tell me, Cedric," Watson broached as they walked behind Holmes. It had been only an hour but it felt much longer. "I am afraid we were not able to get to know each other all that much while you and Alexandra were courting. You were knighted, but Alexandra mentioned you grew up in France?" Watson asked.

"For a time," he answered. "My mother was my father's second wife and a Frenchwoman, as was his first wife. When she died, my father married again but she was a widow with a young son and wanted nothing to do with us. My brother was shipped off to boarding school in Northern England and I was sent to France, where I met Percy and Edmond. I was a year ahead of them but they were welcoming and always... happy, that happiness overflowed to those around them. My brother and I have never been close but Percy and Edmond treated me as their own brother. They finally told me who they were after I had been invited home with them for the holidays. I was the only one in the school who knew their secret. We grew up together. Mrs. Holmes treated me as one of her own sons and when I met Sherlock Holmes, it was one of the best Christmases of my life. I had been staying for the Christmas holiday and he came to visit. My father died a few years ago leaving everything to Gérard and myself."

"Your father was Baron Hughes, was he not?" Watson asked.

"Indeed, Lord Alfred Somers, 7th Baron Hughes," he replied.

"I've heard of him," Watson said. "On a professional level, though, is it your brother who was diagnosed with—"

"My elder brother, Gérard has tuberculosis, yes," he replied.

"I am sorry," Watson said.

"Thank you," he replied. "He is not long for this world, I'm afraid."

"Watson!" Holmes called to him. Watson nodded to Cedric and walked toward Holmes.

"He's a good lad," Watson said. "I misjudged him."

"Who?" Holmes asked.

"Cedric," Watson replied.

"Watson, this is no time for trivialities, look," Holmes pointed his stick toward a dark stain on the ground. "Blood."

Watson crouched down and touched the stain. He rubbed it between his fingers and smelled.

"Yes," he answered standing. "You think this is where he was killed?"

"If it were a butcher shop, I would say the blood is probably normal, but this is a smithy. I would say it is rather interesting, wouldn't you agree?" Holmes asked.

"Well, when you put it like that..." Watson said.

"Have you learned nothing from me, Watson?" Holmes asked. "Cedric," he called him over. "Wait two minutes and then come in after us. You don't know us, understood?"

"Yes, Sir," he answered.

"Good man," Holmes nodded and turned to go into the blacksmith's shop.

The shop was small and the sound of smithing from the back was muted. A boy greeted them.

"Good mornin', gen'lemen," he said. "What can I do for

you?"

"I was actually looking for something quite specific. The wife, you know, she needs something and I have literally been to every retail store with no luck," Watson watched as Holmes disguised himself into a wealthy aristocrat. He lightened his voice to a British Dandy, pulled himself up to his full height and adjusted his posture to be looking down his long nose at the boy. "She saw it at a friend's house and fell in love with it. You're my last hope," Holmes said.

"Well if you would describe it, Sir, perhaps I could help. If we do not have it available, we can have you place an order for it. It would be ready in about a week," the boy explained.

"Oh dear me, no," Holmes said condescendingly. "That will never do. My wife would never forgive me if she had to wait more than three days."

"Well, Sir, we do have a way, it would be rather expensive, but let's see if we could find it in our stock first," the boy offered.

The door opened and Cedric came in.

"Good morning, Sir, I'll be with you in a minute," he said.

"I must say your store is very *écouter et voir ce que vous pouvez apprendre*," Holmes said. Watson understood a little of what he said though it was obviously a message to Cedric. Cedric did not reply. He kept looking around the store.

"Oh... tha — thank you, Sir. I'm not quite sure what that means but Pa and I try hard to keep it fully stocked. Sometimes it seems, what with the needs of gen'leman like yourself, sir and the roughs we have to deal with from time to time, we can't keep it stocked properly," the boy explained leading Holmes to a particular area of the shop.

"Roughs, you say?" Holmes asked acting surprised. "Hmm... thieves?" He clutched his overcoat closer to him as if guarding his pocketbook, even though Watson knew Holmes never carried his pocketbook in his coat.

"Oh, not just that, sir, last night a man was murdered right outside Pa's shop," the boy said excitedly. "We weren't sure if we would be able to open the shop this morning, but when the police came the body was gone!"

"Indeed?" Holmes asked.

"Yes, sir," the boy replied.

"Well, what happened?" Holmes asked in a voice urging the boy to continue.

"I don't know, sir. Pa and I were working late last night and we heard some horses outside. I got to the window and saw a huge black carriage. It was beautiful. Pa came over to me and looked out too. We saw a flash of light from inside the carriage and heard a loud noise even over the sound of the furnace. Pa pulled me back and grabbed his rifle. He told me to stay inside. I looked out of the window and the carriage drove off." The boy explained.

"How exciting!" Holmes replied.

"Oh, it was," he answered.

"What happened to the body?" Watson asked.

"That's just it, sir," the boy said. "Pa came back and said it was there and sent me for the police. But when we got back, the body was gone and Pa was tied up in the back of the shop."

"Fascinating," Holmes said.

"Oh, it was the most exciting thing in me whole life!" he answered. "But let me know what you were looking for, Sir. Pa always says I talk too much."

"Actually, it looks just like this," Holmes grabbed something off the shelf.

"That's a lovely piece, Sir," he said taking it back to the counter. "Would you like me to wrap it up for you?"

"Yes, thank you," Holmes said. "I wonder if you have any *son père ne voyions qui lui a ligoté?*" Again, Watson knew it was a message for Cedric. However, to his credit, Cedric did not react.

"I'm afraid not, Sir, but like I said we can take orders," the boy replied.

"Quite so," Holmes answered. "Well, it's of no great importance."

"That'll be ten shillings," the boy said starting to wrap the piece.

Holmes counted out the money and accepted the parcel.

"Thank you, my boy," Holmes said.

"Thank you, sir," he answered. "I hope your wife will be pleased with it."

"I'm quite sure she will be, and if she needs anything else, well, I know who to go to especially for any *hôtel en face de la rue*," Holmes pulled out a half crown and handed it to the boy. "For your help, my lad. You have saved me my wife's good opinion."

"Thank you kindly, sir!" He breathed out in shock at the money in his hands.

Holmes and Watson left the shop. Watson walked up to his friend as Holmes pulled on his gloves.

"Well, Holmes," Watson said. "I do believe you played that poor boy."

"He'll forgive me, I'm sure," he said. "We at least found out what we needed."

"That the man was shot then his body moved," Watson said.

"And also that the person who supposedly moved the body tied up the blacksmith," Holmes replied.

"Supposedly?" Watson asked. "You forget, I've been your partner for many years. I can catch those subtle words of yours."

"How is it, Watson, that you can catch those words but happen to miss an entire line of deduction?"

"I'm a doctor, Holmes not a detective," he replied. "Now what was all that French nonsense?"

"Nonsense you say?" Holmes said. "Tsk, tsk, tsk, I always forget you have not had the privilege to understand and speak French."

"Well, now, really, Holmes," Watson said.

"It's all right, my dear fellow, how about a pint in the pub across the way? We can wait for Cedric to finish the task I gave him," Holmes said.

Chapter Sixteen

Edmond shut the door behind him and turned to Percy.

"All this knighting talk, I have to say, I feel a thief," Percy said. "This discovery is yours. Not mine."

"Percy," Edmond said. "I wanted you to have the credit. I know how much you wish to establish yourself here."

"Well I must say, I did feel an excitement when they mentioned it," Percy replied.

"So you will soon have a title, a seat in the House and a bit of money to your name," Edmond winked. "A fine catch for any young woman."

Percy chuckled. "Am I that transparent?"

"Oh, *mon cher frère*," Edmond shook his head. "Terribly so."

They both laughed as they walked down the hallway to the scowls of other members.

Holmes ordered two pints from the barman and carried them over to Watson who sat at a table beside the open window.

"Now, Holmes," Watson said as Holmes settled himself into the seat across. "What was all that French about and what did you task Cedric to do?"

"A young man like the blacksmith's son has no qualms about telling a stranger his whole life. But, by nature, there's only so much anyone could ask before he would become suspicious, so, I asked what I could and then needed a confederate who did not look like they were apart of us in order for him to get more information. Enter Cedric, who you have already remarked is a 'good lad'. When he came into the store, I told him to listen and see what he could learn. Then I asked him to get the next bit of information that I was not able to get without stirring the boy's curiosity. I asked him to see if the father remembered who tied him up."

"But if he was going to get that information, then why aren't we waiting for him where he can see us?" Watson asked.

"And risk the young chap knowing we were of the same party? Certainly not! He is perfectly able to see us here, my dear chap, away from any prying eyes," he answered. "There he is now."

Holmes saw Cedric leave the smithy and walk over to the pub. Entering the restaurant, Cedric's eyes scanned the customers for Holmes and Watson. Holmes subtly waved him over. Cedric nodded once and made his way to them.

"How did he know we would be here?" Watson asked.

"Because, my dear doctor, I told him where we would be. If you had but a little more French you would know that," Holmes said. Cedric sat down across from Watson next to Holmes.

"Would you care for a pint, Cedric?" Holmes asked.

"Thank you, no, Mr. Holmes," he answered.

"Did you find out anything?" Holmes asked.

"Well, only one thing, Sir, the boy's father came out of the back and boxed his ears for talking to me," Cedric replied.

"Indeed?" Holmes asked. "That is interesting."

"But I did manage to find out that no one else came

down the street that evening after the murder," he said. "As soon as I started to ask about his father's incident that's when he emerged."

"A large man," Holmes surmised.

"A great brute of a man, Sir. At least three inches taller than me and a good deal larger. He was built like an ox."

Watson gaped at Cedric. He was just as tall as Holmes, but his build was much broader and sheer muscle as Watson had found out the day he tried to drag him out of his house.

"Interesting, and you say the boy's father was upset he was talking to you?" Holmes asked.

"Oh more than upset, Sir," Cedric replied. "He came barreling into the room, fists flying, yelling, cursing some words I had never heard a man say, and then boxed his son's ears," Cedric shook his head. "Can I just say how lucky I am my father was a good man? I am fortunate to have had him and you as my father-figure, sir. I could never imagine treating my own son and heir like that."

"Yes, yes," Holmes replied oblivious to the compliment Cedric had just paid him. As usual, Holmes' focus was only on the case. But Watson did not fail to recognize it.

"Perhaps I misjudged you, Cedric," Watson said softly. Cedric looked over at him.

"I should never have taken that advantage, Doctor," he replied. "For that I am very sorry."

"Very interesting," Holmes took a drink of his ale not having heard anything that just passed between them. "After we finish, I will need to go to Scotland Yard."

"What have you discovered, Holmes?" Watson asked.

"You know my methods," Holmes replied.

"Oh," Watson sighed exasperated. "Can we not do this again? You know I am a hopeless case. Could you just tell me?"

"Nonsense," Holmes replied. "You are becoming quite observant."

"Nevertheless," Watson said. "What did you think of?"

"Could someone have moved the body between the time the boy left for Scotland Yard and when he returned?" Holmes asked.

"Obviously the facts say so," Watson said.

"The facts merely state the body was moved, not who moved it. That is a fact I learned from the boy himself," Holmes replied.

"What are you saying?" Watson asked rubbing his temples feeling a headache coming on.

"The blacksmith moved the body," Holmes said quite simply.

"What?" Watson looked up.

"Well, certainly it's obvious," Holmes said.

"Not to me, sir, he was tied up when they found him," Cedric replied.

"Oh, dear me," Holmes sighed. "You're not there, are you? No, very well then, take it from the beginning. Watson, you are the blacksmith. A body is dumped on your very doorstep, the place you make your livelihood, the carriage that dropped him has driven off not to return. How would you feel?"

"Naturally, I would be very upset," Watson said.

"Understandably, so what do you do?" Holmes asked.

"I would send someone for the police," Watson replied.

"Good, and then?" Holmes prompted.

"Then, nothing, I would wait for them to arrive and perhaps guard the crime scene," Watson said.

"Dear god, you are so absurdly conscientious," Holmes sighed and shook his head.

"Holmes," Watson warned.

Holmes waved him off.

"If you were not so... you," Holmes went on. "You would move the body. Tampering with evidence is much easier to argue away than losing access to your shop for heavens knows how long. You figure no one would be the wiser if you move the body and tie yourself up. That way you are free to do your work and the body is where it belongs, out of your hair." The two men stared uncomprehending. "A great beast of a man tied up? It would take more than just a carriage full of men to do that," Holmes went on. "Therefore, he must have done it himself or been complacent."

"That does make sense, sir, the man's demeanor did convey guilt," he said.

"Quite so," Holmes answered. "I suspected it from the start but I knew I would not have been able to ascertain the truth from him so I spoke with the boy. Now we let Scotland Yard do the rest and we go on looking for the man who pulled the trigger, not the one who moved the body."

"Oh," Cedric looked down.

"Oh?" Holmes asked.

"Forgive me, sir; I just was hoping this would be one of your infamous cases where you had an incredibly brilliant solution, as it is, this seemed absurdly simple."

Watson laughed outright at the indignation on Holmes' face.

"Not every case can be interesting," Holmes answered. "But this one is far from complete," Holmes finished his pint. "Then it's on to Baker Street."

Chapter

Seventeen

Edmond played the E string of his violin. The final note of Chopin's nocturne in c-sharp minor rang out just as Percy finished the chord on the piano.

The brothers looked at each other and smiled. It had been far too long since they had played a duet. Nearly every day while in France they would hone their skills and learn new pieces, always with Percy on the piano and Edmond on the violin. A graduate of the Paris Conservatory in Piano Performance, Percy maintaining his skill along with his brother who was taught violin by their father.

Similarly to their father, the brothers played to focus their minds. This case was weighing heavily on them both. They knew how important this case was, not just to the peerage and the security of the realm but also the fact they had a suspicion who was behind it all.

"Percy, we must discuss something," Edmond started.

"*Oui, mon frere*," Percy replied. "I know."

"I do not believe this murder is a random event and I thoroughly believe there will be more," Edmond said.

"Your theories are similar to my own," Percy answered.

"Then are we similar in another area?" Edmond asked. "Do we both have an idea who is behind this?"

Percy sighed and stood from the piano bench.

"Yes, Edmond," he replied. "I do believe we do."

Holmes and Watson dropped Cedric off at his flat so he could freshen up from his ordeal the previous evening. When they arrived at Baker Street, Marguerite was waiting for them and asked to speak with Sherlock privately for a moment. They stepped into his room and closed the door. Not five minutes later, Watson heard a sharp knock on the study door.

"Ah, Gregson, come in, come in," Watson said when he opened the door. "Sit down, whisky and soda?" Watson offered.

"Oh thank you, doctor, that would be lovely," Gregson said walking over and sitting down.

"Holmes," Watson called. "Gregson's here."

Holmes' door opened and he stepped out followed by Marguerite pinning a hat on her hair.

"Ah, Gregson," Holmes said. "Good man, Watson," he said seeing Watson hand Gregson a drink.

"I shall leave you in peace, Sherlock," Marguerite said finishing her pinning and kissing his cheek. "I am to meet with the Countess of Selborne for tea."

"Of course," he said. "Do be careful."

"Always," she replied. "Good afternoon, gentlemen," she greeted Watson and Gregson. "Oh and Doctor?" she called back. "Do keep an eye on him for me," she winked and swept out of the room. "Now, then, Gregson," Holmes replied changing the subject. "What brings you to Baker Street?"

Pouring himself a whisky and soda, Holmes grabbed a cigarette from his case on the mantle.

"I just wanted to let you know I finished speaking with Miss Austen, the dead man's fiancée," Gregson explained.

"Indeed? Pray, tell us what you discovered," Holmes sat in his armchair.

"Well, there isn't much to say, Sir, Miss Austen is a

pretty, young woman... highly emotional when we explained what happened," Gregson replied.

"The poor girl just lost her fiancé," Watson said.

"She didn't know of anyone who would have wanted Spooner killed," Gregson said.

"Quite so," Holmes replied. "And yet, he had the misfortune of losing every servant he had within two weeks, retaining only a half day maid." Holmes explained.

"How did you–" Gregson started.

"Mrs. Holmes brought it to my attention just a moment ago," Holmes replied. "She had seen it in the paper... the – uh," Holmes chuckled, "gossip column. She thought it was interesting and took a mental note of it."

"I thought you put no stock in the gossip column, Holmes," Watson teased.

"Only when something important is reported," Holmes replied.

"You avoid it like the plague," Watson kept going.

"I do, however my wife..." he took a moment and savored that phrase. "Finds it very entertaining. You know what women are like, Watson."

"I will tell Marguerite you said that," Watson chewed on the end of his pipe.

Holmes shifted uncomfortably.

"I would prefer you did not," Holmes said. Watson's eyes danced with anticipation. "I would like to maintain my sleeping arrangements."

Watson chuckled.

"Every servant within two weeks?" Gregson asked surprising them both by being the only one still focused on the case.

"So it appears. Rebecca was correct in her observations," Watson remarked.

"Quite," Holmes answered. "He had run upon hard times and was forced to let them all go."

"Blyme," Gregson breathed.

"I am guessing, then, you want to go and speak with them?" Watson asked.

"Only one, a man who knows Spooner perhaps better

than his fiancée. A man who would have had his confidence..."

They both stared at Holmes blankly.

"His manservant, of course," Holmes stated. "Really, you two... will you never learn from me? But let's have Percy and Edmond join us."

Chapter Eighteen

"Won't you sit down, Mr. Braxton?" Holmes offered Spooner's former manservant.

"Thank you, sir, but I would rather stand," Braxton, a relatively young man, mid 30s, tall, handsome features, and curly hair answered.

"You know who I am?" Holmes asked.

"Indeed, sir," he answered looking from Holmes to Percy then back again. "But I cannot, for the life of me understand why you have come to me."

"Have you heard your previous employer, Mr. Henry Spooner has been murdered?" Holmes asked. Braxton blinked.

"I think I will need to sit now, sir, if you don't mind," Braxton said.

"Of course," Holmes replied beckoning him to sit in the chair behind him. Percy watched him.

"How long were you working for him, Braxton?" Percy asked.

"I only worked a very short time, sir, three months. He was my first employer as a manservant," Braxton explained. "I was a footman for nearly five years and Mr. Spooner noticed me when he came to visit my previous employer. I looked after Mr. Spooner when he came for a hunting party. A greater master there never was, sir. May I ask, how did he die?"

"He was shot," Holmes said. Braxton visibly cowered.

"'Death is the end of life; ah, why should life all labor be?'" Braxton breathed. Percy's ears pricked up. He had not heard that Tennyson quote in years.

"'Let us alone. Time driveth onward fast, and in a little while our lips are dumb. Let us alone,'" Percy continued the quote. Braxton looked up at him.

"'What is it that will last? All things are taken from us, and become portions and parcels of the dreadful past,'" Braxton said.

"And what portions and parcels did Spooner have of a dreadful past?" Percy asked.

Braxton looked down and took a deep breath.

"Mr. Spooner was a very kind and understanding gentleman. I would rather not speak ill of him," Braxton replied.

"Your loyalty is highly commendable, Braxton," Percy said. "But if we are to figure out why Mr. Spooner was murdered it would be best to tell us as much as you can. You will be breaking no confidences by telling us."

Sighing, Braxton nodded. "Well, sir, one evening, Mr. Spooner rang for me long before his usual time to dress for dinner. When I entered his room, I found him sitting at his bed his head hung low and a letter clutched in his hand. I asked him if everything was all right and he told me..."

"Yes," Percy coaxed.

"He told me he was a dead man... a ruined, dead man. He said he had massive debts that he had no way of paying. He told me he would have to make the announcement to the rest of the staff later. He had enough to pay us a fortnight's wages but after that he would not be able to retain our services. He said he would write sterling letters of recommendation for all of us and see to it we were placed within that time. He was a good master and a good man, sir."

"Did he tell you to whom he owned money?" Holmes

asked.

"No, sir," he answered.

"You are employed now though," Percy speculated.

"As head footman, sir," he answered. "My current employer has no need of a manservant."

"What duties did you perform for Mr. Spooner, Braxton?" Percy asked.

"I was his manservant, sir, but I also acted as his butler. I dressed him, waited at table, took his callers and ran the household," Braxton explained.

"How many in the household?" Percy asked.

"About half a dozen, sir," he answered. "As a bachelor he had little need for a large staff."

"And now you're just a footman?" Percy asked shaking his head. "A waste."

"This is a good house, sir, I am well provided for. I have no complaints," he said.

"Indeed," Percy replied.

"Braxton," Holmes' tone indicated that he was tired of this line of questioning. "Do you know of anyone who had a grudge against your previous employer? Did anything untoward happen?"

"No, sir... Well," he continued as if he just remembered something. "There was one thing."

"And what was that?" Holmes asked.

"I did not mean to overhear, but voices were raised," Braxton started.

"Go on," Holmes said.

"Mr. Spooner was in a heated argument with another man a few days before he told me he was going to have to let everyone go," Braxton explained. "He said something about making good on debts made. My understanding was the man owed him some money."

"Did you hear anything else?" Holmes asked. "Do you know who the man was?"

"Mr. Spooner said he needed the money that was promised to him but the man replied and said his solicitors had cut him off without a penny for a time. It was up to his brother to pay him back. My French is not that good, sir."

"French?" Holmes asked. "They were speaking in French?"

"Oh yes, sir, my understanding was the man went to school with Mr. Spooner," Braxton said. "I believe they did not want anyone to know of what they were speaking."

"Do you know the name of the man he was speaking with?" Holmes asked.

"I believe he called him Somers, sir and another time I heard the name Gérard," Braxton replied.

Holmes did not react. Nodding, he extended his card to Braxton.

"If you recall anything else, be sure to let me know," Holmes said.

"Of course, Sir," Braxton replied. "Allow me to see you to the door."

After Braxton escorted them out, Holmes turned to Percy who was pulling on his gloves.

"Why do I get the feeling you were interviewing him, Percy?" Holmes asked.

"Was I?" Percy shrugged. "Dear me," he teased. "I do not intend on staying with Cedric forever, now do I? And when I do move, I will need someone to run the household."

"Quite so," Holmes answered.

"Holmes, who the devil was he talking about?" Watson asked. "Cedric's name is not Gérard."

"No, but his elder brother's is," Holmes answered. "I need to speak with Cedric about this. I have serious doubts he knew anything about his brother's debts, but he may be able to speak with his solicitors."

"Baker Street?" Percy asked.

"Quite so," Holmes replied.

"Mr. Holmes," A uniformed policeman came running up to him. "Very sorry sir, but there is a message from Inspector Lestrade. Sir, he asks you and anyone you deem trustworthy to come to the West End. There's been another development."

"Another development?" Holmes asked. "Who has been found this time?"

"I do not know, sir," the man replied. "Will you come?"

Holmes looked at Percy and Watson who both nodded.

"We shall," he said.

"Constable, did Inspector Lestrade ask for me?" Gregson asked.

"I only had Mr. Holmes' name, sir," he answered.

"Thank you," Gregson replied.

"Care to come along, Gregson?" Holmes offered.

"No, thank you, Mr. Holmes," Gregson answered. "I had better be getting back to the Yard. I should write up Mr. Braxton's statement and enter it in the file. There's a lot of paperwork, gentlemen. Police work will always win out in the end."

"But this could have something to do with the case at hand," Percy replied.

"I doubt it, sir," he answered. "It was two completely different sections of town. No, I will find our criminal. All it takes is a little deduction. We'll soon have our man."

"Well, if I can help in anyway, Gregson, let me know," Holmes said, his sarcasm heavily veiled.

"Thank you, Mr. Holmes, but like I said this is police work. We'll soon have our man," Gregson walked down the road and hailed a cab. Percy turned to his father.

"He really thinks this isn't connected?" Percy asked.

"I think he doesn't want this to be connected," Holmes replied. "If it is, that means Lestrade, the senior officer, will have control over this case and Gregson is passed over again."

"Ah," Percy replied. "And all his police work will be in vain."

"Quite so," Holmes stated.

"You think it is connected, do you not, father?" Percy asked.

"Of course," he answered. "But I'll know more when I see what little evidence is left after the police have trampled through it all. Come along."

"Should we send a note to Edmond?" Percy asked.

"I have no way of knowing where he is, and I do believe he already knows," Holmes said hailing a cab.

Chapter Nineteen

The cab came to a stop just outside a rundown building. Holmes got out and headed to the officer standing by the door. Percy and Watson followed slowly after him.

"What occupation do you foresee yourself undertaking, Percy?" Watson asked out of the blue. Percy looked over surprised. "I overheard you and Holmes speaking about that footman."

"Well, sir, I do have a bit of money stored away. My father's mother was a lady and on my twenty-first birthday, I came into a little money. Enough to set myself up. I have always had an interest in British politics, perhaps... well, that is a far-off dream," Percy replied.

"What is?" Watson asked.

"Well, I have always been interested in the ambassadorship to France," Percy replied.

"Indeed?" Watson asked. "What did you study at University?"

"I went to the *Conservatoire de Paris* and studied piano performance alongside Maurice Ravel, perhaps you've heard of him? I also studied politics; both are passions," Percy replied.

"Hmm," Watson said. "Would you have the sufficient income to support a wife and family?"

"For now. I have one thousand pounds a year, it is a sufficient income for moderate tastes and if I am fortunate enough to secure an appointment with the government, I expect to at least double, if not triple that income."

Watson nodded slowly.

"Are you two quite finished?" Holmes drolled from the doorway.

"Sorry, Holmes," Watson replied. "I'm just getting to know your son."

"Yes, so I've observed," Holmes answered. "Lestrade is waiting for us."

The three of them walked into the shabby building, the stench causing Percy to cough and his body to react.

"Dear God, what is that stench?" Percy groaned.

"Human decay," a familiar voice came from the darkness. Edmond walked over to them.

"Ah excellent, I hoped you were here," Holmes said.

"I was visiting mother and Rebecca when Lestrade's message arrived," Edmond explained. "I told his man where to find you and offered to come myself."

"Well then, since you were here before us, what did you observe?" Holmes asked.

"I requested the police leave all as it was, and to permit no one but myself and Inspector Lestrade into the room," Edmond replied.

"Is this the same?" Holmes asked.

"I believe so," Edmond replied. "The man has the symbol for *collapse* carved into his forehead."

"Excellent," Holmes said. "Lead on, Ed."

They followed Edmond through the stench of opium mixed with human decay to a door.

"The gambling den is through here," Edmond replied.

"Poor fellow," Watson breathed when he saw the corpse seated in a chair, slumped over the table.

"How could any man do this?" Percy asked. "It's despicable."

"Yes, it is, but it is also one more stepping stone to the truth," Edmond said.

"Do we have a name?" Holmes asked.

"No, sir, not yet," Edmond replied. "We're in the process of locating the proprietor; perhaps he will be able to tell us more."

Raised voices at the door drew their attention. Edmond moved away and went to the Chinese man and the policeman. Holmes followed.

"It's all right, constable," Edmond said. "The man doesn't speak English." Looking at the other man, Edmond began speaking to him in Chinese. After a few moments, he turned back to the rest of them.

"This man is the proprietor. He has no idea who that man is," Edmond explained. "He left for lunch and no one was here, then he returned and saw the police. He is just as confused as we are."

Holmes motioned the man over and showed him the body and asked him a question, also in Chinese.

"This man has never been here before," Holmes translated after a short conversation. "I have some research to do. I will be at the London Library. Edmond, I could use your help. You two, feel free to return to Baker Street. I will join you tonight."

The gigantic building, home to the London Library, mesmerized Edmond. There was nothing he loved more than books. The musty smell assaulted his nose and his fingers ached to hold a book.

Veering off to another door opening to a corridor, Edmond walked silently beside his father. Holmes slowed and turned to another door. When he opened it, they were in a large round room that looked much smaller than it was due to the amount of books cluttering the shelves. The domed roof was many feet above them and gave way to another floor of books that overlooked the one they were in. There was no one else in the room apart from one librarian. Holmes went up to her. She peered over her glasses as they approached.

"Oh, good day, Mr. Holmes," she greeted. She was a small, hunched, prematurely gray-haired woman.

"Miss White, allow me to introduce, my son, Edmond Holmes," Holmes gestured to Edmond beside him.

"A pleasure, Mr. Holmes," she breathed. Edmond gave a stiff bow. "I read about you of course. I was telling my sister, Marjorie, just the other day while I was reading about you, that nice Mr. Holmes is such a good looking young man, I was sure he would have numerous women hoping he would be interested in them. And I told her, 'Marjorie,' I said. 'I am certain his sons will be just as handsome'. I see I am not wrong."

Edmond smiled slightly and bowed again. "You are too kind," he said.

"Oh and that accent!" She gushed. "I always had a *penchant* for French accents. Are there any young woman you are particularly interested in at the moment?"

Edmond swallowed and for some reason the book *Great Expectations* came to his mind.

"No, not at the moment, ma'am," he said.

"Oh?" She sounded hopeful. Edmond tried to suppress his urge to run away. "Then perhaps you would take tea with my sister and me sometime soon?"

"I am sure Edmond would love to, Miss White," Holmes answered and Edmond had to bite his lips to prevent his groan escaping as he looked over at his father. The woman was old enough to be his grandmother. "You know how much I always enjoy speaking with you, Miss White, but we are currently on a vital task from the government and we need to utilize the library," Holmes said. "Is there any way my son and I could be left alone for a few hours?"

She looked from Edmond to Holmes then back again.

"I am certain that should not be a problem, as long as I have Mr. Holmes' word he will join my sister and me for tea as soon as this exciting case is over," she said. Holmes looked over at his son.

"Well go on, Ed," Holmes teased. Edmond began coughing. "Poor boy, he's not been feeling well," Holmes turned back to Miss White.

"Oh, dear me," she cried.

"It's this London air," Edmond choked out.

"Well, let me get you a cuppa," she offered sliding off the stool and straightening the front of her wool dress. "It is almost tea time anyway." She walked around the large desk, and with a final look at Edmond, left the room.

"Hoo," Edmond let out.

"Really, Ed," Holmes grinned. "You should contain yourself, such excitement is not good for poor old Miss White." Holmes barely got the words out before he began laughing.

"Miss Havisham more like," Edmond replied.

Holmes barked with laughter. "Very like indeed," he replied.

"And you tossed me to her without mercy," Edmond said. "I will not forget that in a hurry."

"All for the case, *mon fils*," Holmes winked.

"Of course," Edmond replied chuckling.

"Now, shall we get to work?" Holmes asked.

Edmond nodded and followed his father down the many aisles. Finally, when Holmes found what he was looking for he pulled out book after book and stacked them on Edmond's outstretched arms. After Holmes had almost buried his son in old books, they walked to the reading desks and sat opposite each other. Edmond sneezed as he lowered the books to the desk.

"What exactly are we looking for, Sir?" Edmond asked taking one of the books and flipping it open.

"Any mention of those words; balance and collapse," Holmes said.

Edmond nodded, knowing there could be hundreds but also realizing what context his father was thinking, he turned to the books and divided them between them.

It was about two hours later when Edmond called to his father.

"Dad," he said. Holmes looked over at him. "Look at this."

Edmond passed him the book with his finger on what he wanted his father to see.

"Collapse... balance," Holmes read. "This is the story of the Great Wall of China." Edmond nodded. "And if I'm reading this right, your Chinese is better than mine, but I see there are more words, meaning there are going to be more murders," Holmes said.

"All the original markings on the wall at the six points," Edmond said.

Holmes kept reading. His brows furrowed. "This doesn't match with —" he stopped himself.

"With what, Dad?" Edmond asked.

"Nothing," Holmes said. "Just a theory I was formulating, this doesn't correlate with it."

"You always said your first theory is the one you should heed and anything that makes no sense later is just someone trying to confuse you or you're over thinking it," Edmond said.

"You're right," Holmes looked over at his son. "But I have also mentioned, it is a capital mistake to theorize before you have all the data; and there are two equally possible scenarios for this case," Holmes checked his pocket watch. "Ten to six. We should be getting back to Baker Street."

Holmes gathered his things and headed for the door. He stopped when he realized Edmond was not beside him. Turning back, he saw his son still sitting at the desk.

"What is it?" Holmes asked.

"Forgive me, sir," Edmond started. "But what are you not telling me?"

"What makes you think I am holding something back?" Holmes asked.

"Your demeanor," Edmond replied standing. "You have always been open with us, not at all like the clam Dr. Watson portrays you as in his fiction. But with this case you seem to be deliberately trying to keep us... *me,* in the dark. Did I do something?"

"No, not at all, son," Holmes sighed. "There are times when a father feels the need to protect his children. Even though you are a grown man, you will always be my son and I will always want to protect you. Just know this, if it becomes essential for me to tell you, I will absolutely tell you what I am thinking. But until I deem it necessary, understand I only want to protect you."

"I appreciate that, dad, but... if you would trust me to take care of myself and take me into your confidence, perhaps I could be of some benefit to you," Edmond said.

"You are of more benefit than you know," Holmes replied. "Trust me on this, son. Let me do this my way."

Edmond took a deep breath but stopped his line of inquiry.

"Understood," he said.

Holmes turned away from him and closed his eyes for a moment. He knew Edmond had an idea what was going on but for his safety, Holmes deliberately kept him in the dark.

Chapter Twenty

"Another murder... read all about it... another Boxer murder, get your paper," the boy cried outside Pall Mall. Edmond looked down into his glass of brandy and swirled the contents.

"Another murder," he said looking back out the window.

"Is that what the boy is saying?" Mycroft looked up lazily. "I never can understand them nowadays."

"They're calling it the Boxer Murderer."

"Humph," Mycroft grunted. "The killer is no more Chinese than you or I — well more me than you."

The corner of Edmond's mouth ticked up, but his demeanor changed and he sighed. "Sometimes I feel like a child of two worlds and those worlds are colliding."

"Don't get metaphysical on me, my lad, you know I can't stand all that mumbo-jumbo," Mycroft replied.

"Sorry, Uncle," he said. "But it is true."

"I know it is," Mycroft said softly understanding. "But your home is here now."

When Edmond said nothing, Mycroft stood and walked over to him.

"I do not believe I will ever truly embrace my English heritage. It is just not in my beliefs," Edmond finally answered.

"You believe then it is right what's going on over there?" Mycroft prodded gently. "The killing of innocents?"

"*Non*," Edmond answered. "Killing of anything is something no one should condone, but especially the killing of human beings. But I do believe every country has its own right to be independent. Look at the Americas. They have set up a thriving bureaucracy in just a couple centuries. No, sir, I cannot condone what the Boxers are doing, but I do understand why they are doing it."

"Well, so can I, but is it not our right also, to go and defend the innocent men and women who are being murdered?" Mycroft asked.

Edmond said nothing. He was the only one in his family who did not agree with the British Empire.

"Forgive me if I have given offence," he said.

"Not in the least, we are all entitled to our own opinion," his uncle said. "But perhaps when you speak to the queen again, you keep your personal beliefs to yourself, eh my boy? I know several men at the Home Office who would challenge you to a duel for those words."

"I will strive not to embarrass you," Edmond conceded.

"You never could," Mycroft replied. He put a hand on his nephew's shoulder in a fatherly reassurance.

"I wonder who has been killed this time," Edmond went on as Mycroft stepped away from the window back to the fire.

"We should have been called if there was anything of importance," Mycroft said. "If there is, wake me, my boy, would you? I'll retire to my room."

"Of course. Good night, Uncle," Edmond said.

"Good night to you, my lad," Mycroft replied as he walked out of the door.

Edmond turned from the window and looked around the empty room. The study was just as one would expect for a bachelor living on his own. Mycroft took little pride in decorating, but he did take care to have a place where he could entertain his frequent political guests.

Edmond finished the rest of his brandy and set the glass down on the tea cart behind the armchair his uncle so frequently lounged in. Gently touching the book his uncle had set out, Edmond read the title and author. Charles Dickens was not one of Edmond's favorite authors, but it was a good choice. He walked around the room stopping by the fireplace, absently twisting the ring on the smallest finger of his right hand that had been a gift from his father when he became of age. Both he and his brother wore the ring with the engraved H their father had given them on their fifteenth birthday and Rebecca had a pendant with the same design. It always grounded him and helped him think.

This case was a muddle. He was not at all certain what was going on. All he knew was this felt too close. Something was off.

He felt the hair on the back of his neck stand on end. Someone was watching him. His eyes darted to the window. Looking out, through the rain drop streaked window pane, he locked eyes with a man across the way in the other flat. The man immediately looked away and walked from the window. Edmond's shrewd sense of human nature took control. Who was that man and why was he in a house that had been vacant for more than a month and no one had mentioned anything of it being let out to a man in his mid to late 30s. Edmond rang the bell calling the servant. He watched the road and the window to see if the man appeared in either location.

The maid knocked on the door and, at Edmond's beckoning, walked in.

"You called for me, sir?" she asked.

"Ah, Rachel, you were friends with the young maid who worked across the way before her master and mistress closed up the house for the season, were you not?" He asked.

"Yes, sir," she answered.

"Do you recall her mentioning her master letting the rooms to anyone while they were gone?" He asked.

"Why, no, sir," she replied. "I remember she said he had offers but he was a proud man and refused them all, if you'll forgive me saying that, sir."

"So, you know of no reason why anyone would be living in that house across the street right now?" Edmond asked.

"None at all, sir," she replied.

"Thank you, Rachel, could you go to my uncle and wake him, tell him I have gone over to check on something and I will need to speak to him immediately when I return," Edmond ordered.

"Of course, sir. I wish you would be careful, sir," she said.

"I can take care of myself, Rachel, have no worry," he replied.

"Should I call for the police, sir?" she asked.

"No," he answered pulling on his coat. "Do not call for the police until my uncle or I tell you to, understand?"

"Yes, sir," she answered. "Sir, you had better take your scarf, it is frightfully cold out there."

"I'll be all right," he replied. "Wake him immediately after I leave."

"Yes, sir," she answered.

Chapter

Twenty-One

As Edmond finally opened the door to the study an hour and a half later, he was soaked to the bone. Mycroft stood pacing in front of the fire and looked up sharply when his nephew walked in.

"Dammit, man don't you know how worried I have been?" Mycroft demanded as soon as he walked in.

"Forgive me, Uncle, I had to check something," Edmond said shaking out of his wet coat. Rachel went up to him and took his coat. Taking out the newspaper he had in the pocket, he thanked her.

"So I was told," Mycroft harrumphed. "But confound it man, couldn't you let the police do their job?"

"I am perfectly ready for the police to do their job, Uncle, but I wanted to look the place over first," Edmond said unbuttoning his vest and collar. He took off his vest and handed it to Rachel as well. Going over to the fire, he dismissed her. After she left the room, Edmond began pulling off his boots.

"You are soaked through," Mycroft said.

"I am aware of that fact, Uncle," Edmond looked up at him. "And as I'm sure you do not wish for me to catch my death you will, I'm sure, forgive me if I take the nonessential clothing off."

"Do what you must," Mycroft replied. With a nod of thanks, Edmond unbuttoned his shirt and cuffs. "What did you see?"

He poured his nephew a glass of brandy to warm him.

"I felt someone watching me and looked out the window. I saw a man standing directly across from me watching this flat. I asked Rachel about it and she said there was to be no one renting that house while the owners were away for the spring. So I went over to see who the man was. When I arrived, I found the bird flown but I did see some very distinctive tobacco. I took a sample for Father to analyze –"

He was cut off by his uncle's gasp. Edmond turned to see what was wrong. Mycroft was staring at his bare back.

"What is it?" Edmond asked.

"Your back," Mycroft breathed. "You have... scars."

Edmond looked at him. "I was in the Orient for eight years, Uncle," he said cautiously. "I have plenty of scars."

"It looks like you were..."

"Whipped?" Edmond offered. "I was."

"What? Why?" Mycroft demanded meeting his eyes.

"Discipline," Mycroft could tell he was lying. "I travelled home soon after."

"Will you not tell me what happened?"

"Forgive me, I find it... too raw to speak of as yet," he turned away but not before Mycroft saw a glistening tear in his eye. "If it bothers you I can put my shirt back on."

"No, no it's all right," he said. "It startled me, is all."

"Forgive me for not warning you," Edmond replied. "I have forgotten about it."

Instead of pressing the matter, Mycroft changed the subject. "You have a tattoo on your back, Chinese symbols, what does it say?" Mycroft asked.

"It is my rank and name," he replied. "Rank in the martial arts and the name I chose while I was over there."

"What was that?" Mycroft asked.

"I cannot say," he answered. He sat and pulled off his wet socks and rolled up his pant legs. He took a napkin from the tea cart and dried his face, arms, chest, and hair. "I should be dry soon enough," he said accepting the brandy from his uncle. "Thank you. So, I found the tobacco ash and took a sample. I must have just missed him because I could still smell the strong scent of the cigar he was smoking. As soon as I knew there was nothing else to be observed, I went to the bobby at the end of the street and told him what had happened. I gave my name and your address as my residence for now. He went to investigate and will let me know if he discovers anything. Then I went to the local newspaper boy and purchased this paper."

"Who do you think the man was?" Mycroft asked.

"Well, sir I have honestly no idea, but Father's case involving Colonel Sebastian Moran kept coming to my mind but I knew that couldn't be who it was, but then... I thought of *him*."

"Moriarty," Mycroft said.

"I did, sir," he answered.

"Perfectly sound logic, except the man is dead," Mycroft replied.

"Is he?" Edmond asked. "Father climbed out, couldn't he have done something similar?"

"Where would he have been for all these years?" Mycroft asked. "And your father would not lie."

"I never thought he would. As to where he has been, I cannot say," he replied. "It is only a feeling. I have no evidence."

They were both silent for a while.

"Anything interesting in the paper?" Mycroft asked.

"There has been another murder. This is the third one..." Edmond opened it and read. "It appears he was found near a house of ill fame they have no cause of death currently."

"Nothing remotely unusual about that," Mycroft said.

"Quite, however it appears this man had a symbol carved into his forehead..."

"Just like the others," Mycroft started toward his nephew. "Is there a print of it?"

"Yes," he answered. "It's hard to make it out, clearly

whoever wrote this article did not have access to a translator. But having found a connection in the research father and I did at the library," Edmond squinted at the image. "It appears to be the symbol for... mortality."

"Mortality?" Mycroft asked. "How strange."

"Indeed," Edmond replied. "I am also curious as to why we were not asked to investigate the scene."

"Well, my lad, they are called houses of ill fame for a reason," Mycroft replied. "Perhaps they wanted it all cleared up without fuss."

"Without fuss?" Edmond questioned. "Uncle..."

"We can go and speak with your father tomorrow, my lad, but now you should get yourself to bed," Mycroft said. Edmond sighed.

"As much as I wish to go over there tonight, I know you're right and I have become very tired. I will take the main stairs if I may, I do not want to give Rachel a shock," he pulled his shirt from the drying rack in front of the fire. He pulled it on and buttoned a couple buttons letting it hang loose on him.

"She is sweet on you," Mycroft said. "You should have seen her when she told me you left."

Edmond paused at the door. "I know," he replied. "I do not wish to cause her pain and if I have done anything to encourage her, I am sorry. I am not interested in anything at this time."

"A man always has interests, Edmond," Mycroft said. "You are young and many would say handsome, why shouldn't you indulge in life a little?"

"I am sorry, Uncle," he shook his head. "That is not my desire."

Mycroft nodded slowly. "Who was she?" he asked.

Edmond froze but before he answered, he merely gathered his boots and socks, said good night to his uncle and left the room.

Mycroft sat smoking a cigar, thinking. He wanted to know more about the girl who had captured his nephew's heart and what happened to her. Edmond clearly did not desire anyone else.

Turning his thoughts to Edmond's deduction, he pulled

out a cigarette. Both he and Sherlock had hoped Edmond would not think of Moriarty, but that had been floating around their minds for days. They had discussed it one evening out of ear shot of his family. Holmes thought it logical and Mycroft hated what it was doing to his brother, tearing him apart inside. Though Holmes had said nothing at the time, Mycroft could read it in his brother's face when he turned to look at Marguerite laughing and talking with Rebecca and Cedric.

Mycroft sat until the small hours of the morning thinking. He wanted to have another theory come to mind before dawn broke but unfortunately, the more he went over the evidence, the more it pointed to the Napoleon of Crime and the more he hated himself for thinking it. He would have to speak to Sherlock in the morning. That was a conversation he loathed to have.

Chapter

Twenty-Two

"Well, now," Holmes started taking a seat opposite his brother. Edmond stood beside Mycroft. "What brings you both to Baker Street at such an early hour?"

"Forgive us for calling so early, Father," Edmond started.

"Nonsense, Ed," Holmes answered smirking, drawing on his cigarette. "You know time means little to me. What is it that concerns you?"

"There was an interesting... event last night," Edmond continued. "I was all for coming to see you immediately however —"

"I told the boy he needed a good night's sleep after being soaked through, though I'm sure he slept little," Mycroft admitted.

"So I observe," Holmes replied. "Edmond, you do have a tendency to not take care of yourself."

"A habit I learned from someone very close to me," Edmond answered.

"Touché," he said. "But you are here now so tell me,

what have you discovered?"

Edmond told his father about the man he had seen across the street and what he found when he went over to the house. Taking out the envelope of tobacco ash, Edmond described the very pungent odor he smelled when he entered the home.

"I found this on the floor and window ledge. I was hoping you could identify the type and it might shed some light on who this man was," Edmond explained.

Holmes stood and took the envelope from his son.

"Hmm," Holmes said sniffing. "Well done, Edmond. It's Turkish and rather expensive." He walked to his chemicals and started some sort of concoction.

"Also, sir," Edmond said. "There has been another murder, a man was found outside a house of ill fame and had the symbol for mortality carved into his forehead. Were you able to investigate that?"

Holmes turned to look at his son.

"No," Holmes answered. "I was not informed about it until it was too late to discover anything. Even then we know it revolves around the murder of Spooner. I very much doubt there would be any evidence left to collect. I did have a rather strong conversation with Lestrade regarding my investigation. He knows to never keep me in the dark again."

Edmond nodded and yawned. "Take a seat, Edmond, lie down and rest. This will take some time and from the look of it you did not get a good night's sleep last night."

Edmond nodded and lay down on the sofa. He was asleep within minutes. Standing, Mycroft took a blanket and covered his nephew. Holmes nodded his thanks.

"Sherlock," Mycroft walked over to his brother. "I must speak with you about something else that happened. Edmond mentioned something last night and I did not know exactly how you would have wished me to respond."

"And what did he mention?" Holmes asked focusing on the beakers in his hands.

Mycroft did not speak for a moment, only stared at his brother's profile as he worked. Feeling the full weight of his brother's stare, Holmes sighed and put his instruments down, his eyes drifted to his son.

"I hoped he wouldn't have thought of that," he whispered.

"He is a brilliant lad," Mycroft said. "Of course he's going to come to the same realization we did two weeks ago."

Holmes sighed again. "Did he say anything else?"

Mycroft shook his head. "But did you know he has scars on his back? Massive scars? He said he was whipped," Mycroft said.

"Yes, he has told me of their origin, but I will not break his confidence."

"So, it was a woman then?"

"You are entitled to your views. I say nothing," Holmes replied. "That is not important right now. What is, is that he said Moriarty."

"He did not say it, he implied it," Mycroft replied.

"Then how do you know that's what he meant?" Holmes asked. "What exactly happened?"

"Sherlock," Mycroft said. "I know it's what he meant just like you knew it is what I meant a mere moment ago. He didn't actually say the name, he said *him*. I do not know of anyone else who deserves that title. When he did not say it, I voiced the name and he told me it was a theory he had been formulating for some time."

"Why on earth would you say the name? You could have dissuaded him," Holmes hissed.

"I know he must be discouraged to continue," Mycroft replied. "But what else was I supposed to do?"

Holmes sighed. "You are right. The more we discourage him, the more he will gravitate to it... you remember how I was at twenty-three," Holmes said.

"Cannot forget," Mycroft snorted. "No, meant yes to you when it came to investigations."

"Still does," Holmes answered. "Let me think for a while... I must work."

Mycroft nodded and started back to his chair.

"Did you see the man Edmond went after?" He asked.

"No," Mycroft replied turning back to him. "But when Rachel told me Edmond was going across the street without help... well, you know how I care for him."

"Indeed," Holmes answered. "And I am grateful. I never wanted to be as our father was. I hope I have treated both the same and well."

"They have always sung your praises. Edmond and Percy have both told me how they care for you, love you. They have no complaints. You are nothing like our father."

"No," he smiled slightly. "I had a better mentor..." he glanced at Mycroft. His brother stared at him for a moment. "We irk each other often... what brothers do not?" Holmes went on. "But I am thankful for how you became the father to me, we never had."

"Sherlock," Mycroft said softly. "Those chemicals you are working with... are they hallucinogenic?"

"No," he chuckled. "It needed to be said... especially with Moriarty rearing his head again. Why can't he just die? I am tired of looking over my shoulder, being unable to protect my family. Now my family is here, I-"

"Quite," Mycroft put a hand on his brother's shoulder. "Once more into the breach, Sherlock; time to break his curse."

Taking a deep breath, Holmes nodded and looked back at his chemicals.

"It's Latakia," Holmes said seeing the reaction of the tobacco ash.

"That's not very popular," Mycroft replied.

"No, it's not and goes for a half crown per ounce," Holmes explained. "I still have some of the quarter pound you gave me for Christmas. It's some of the finest."

"So the man Edmond saw is wealthy," Mycroft replied.

"It should help us identify our suspect when we catch him," Holmes said.

"Did Moriarty smoke that?" Mycroft asked.

"No," Holmes answered.

"That's a relief," he replied.

"Did you find anything, Father?" Edmond raised himself from the sofa.

His father and uncle looked over at him.

"Were you able to sleep?" Holmes asked suspicious if he overheard their conversation.

"For the most part," Edmond looked into his father's eyes and Holmes knew he had heard enough.

"I did figure out the type of tobacco," Holmes said.

"Excellent," Edmond stood and walked over. They were silent for a little while until Edmond looked over at Holmes. "Dad, if you wish me to not investigate this case as you said, all you need do is to tell me. I will honor you and know there is a reason. I may not like it... but I will stop."

"Your uncle and I worry about the end result of all this," Holmes explained. "My only wish is you and Percy were never drawn into this."

"If you feel like you have failed to keep us safe, Dad, let me assure you nothing could be further from the truth," Edmond said. "Percy and I are fully aware this man could be Moriarty and considering what we know of him, we are not going to go about this on our own. I am truly sorry if I caused either of you unrest because of my rash response. Only know, dad, I wish to be of help, not a hindrance."

Holmes gently placed a hand on his son's face cupping his jaw.

"I know, son," he answered. "You have to understand, my one mission has been to keep you all safe from him. Now he is facing us and I feel I am tied to a chair watching him in a room with you, Percy, and especially your Mother and Rebecca, and I can do nothing to stop him. I could never live with myself if something happened to you."

"No, sir, I know that not to be true," Edmond replied. "You would become, once more, the machine Dr. Watson wrote you to be and you would not rest until his blood flowed through your fingers. You would hunt him down and kill him. I know. Believe me, I know. But until we get this monster, would it not be prudent to work together? We are strongest together. It is a force he can never overcome."

"You are absolutely right," Holmes said. "So tell me your theories."

Chapter Twenty-Three

Holmes woke to a clap of thunder, light dancing across the dark sky and rain pelting the window. Looking beside him, Marguerite was fast asleep. He eased his arm out from under her head. She moaned and turned over. He walked out to the study and Edmond looked up from reading a book in the armchair.

"Everything all right, Dad?" he asked.

"What are you doing up?" Holmes asked softly.

"I couldn't sleep," he answered. "I wanted to make sure all was well."

"Does your uncle know you're here and not in your room?" He asked.

"I spoke with him at dinner," Edmond explained. It had been three days since Edmond brought his father the tobacco ash and during those days Edmond barely slept at night. He stayed on guard making certain his family was safe.

Holmes went to the mantle and lit a cigarette. Edmond accepted the Turkish and lit it, taking a deep draw on the tobacco. Father and son sat opposite each other calmly smoking.

"So," Holmes finally broke the silence. "How about you tell me what's bothering you?"

"I know you've noticed my unusual behavior, Father, but nothing is bothering me. I just feel there is something looming over us and I cannot rid myself of that suspicion." Edmond explained.

Holmes breathed in on his cigarette and nodded.

"I agree," he replied slowly breathing out the smoke. "I feel it too. It is a sense we are cursed with."

Edmond did not speak for a long moment.

"If we look at the facts, sir," he started. "This case lacks one thing... consistency in victims. We have no tie whatsoever between the three so far. Spooner was a man who was badly in debt as we came to know and steals a document from a Home Office agent. He is later found with the papers intact, but he is dead. And his death blatantly points to the serial killer caught almost a year ago.

"Next, we have a man who had no reason for being in the West End, die in a gambler's room in a secret chamber of an Opium den. He never played cards in his life before, not even with friends. His body was found mutilated with the Chinese symbol for collapse carved into his forehead. Then thirdly, we have another man killed outside a whore house with the Chinese symbol for mortality carved into his head. Has anything been discovered? Has Inspector Lestrade gotten in touch with you at all?"

"Nothing yet," Holmes answered. "Dr. Watson may have stretched the truth when it came to me as I'm sure you know, but when he wrote about the good inspector, he was absolutely accurate. All that is known is that he was one of the Boxer's murders. The symbol carved in his forehead tells us that much. Nothing else is known. Not his identity, what he was doing in that place, or why he was killed. As for the other victim from West End, there is no information as to where he was going, where he was coming from, nothing."

"I do not believe the police report that this is random. Those symbols carved into all three of the men's foreheads suggests to me the perpetrator wants to cause panic, and for the blame to be placed on the Boxers while he sits back and watches," Edmond theorized.

"He could be funding both sides of the war, you mean?" Holmes summarized his son's thoughts.

"Exactly," he continued. "It is a dastardly plot. He thinks the war is ending and wants to make sure it continues as long as possible in order for him to get money from it."

"A dastardly plot indeed," Holmes replied. "One might almost say worthy of the Napoleon of Crime..." Holmes' voice trailed off as he watched his son's reaction.

"So you do believe Moriarty is behind this? Could he have survived Reichenbach?" Edmond asked with hardly any emotion. Holmes stood and walked to the fire.

"It is a theory I have been formulating for some time now," he said.

"But how?" Edmond asked.

"I do not know, yet," he answered. "But as you thought, is it so improbable Moriarty was able to climb out of that abyss? It has been done before, you know."

"But years later? To reveal himself in such an obvious manner? And especially now?" Edmond questioned.

"You forget, son, it is obvious only to us," Holmes said. "Maybe that is how he wants it. As for the timing, perhaps he was waiting for such an occasion. He has always been well informed of my life."

They were quiet for a time until Edmond spoke again.

"There are going to be more murders," he stated.

"I guarantee it," Holmes said.

"And there is nothing we can do?" Edmond asked.

"We know who's behind this," Holmes replied. "Three deaths so far... god only knows how many more there will be. He has had ample time to rebuild his army. If we go after him now we will only get a subordinate. What good would that do? I have studied and followed this man for three decades. If I have learned anything about him in that time, it's that he never tells one person the complete picture."

"But capture enough at once you can fit the picture together from their puzzle pieces," Edmond offered.

"To what end?" Holmes asked. "The moment they are

captured even before, he will change the plan. And we'll be back to where we started."

"Then there is nothing to do but wait and hope he contacts us," Edmond said.

"Not us... me," Holmes replied. "I'm not involving you or your mother in this."

"We are already involved, Father," Edmond said. "It started the moment you fell in love with her."

Holmes paused, his eyes fixed on his son.

"Let us help you..." Edmond stood and walked over to his father. He stood close to him. "Let *me* help you..."

Holmes' grey eyes never left his son's. "If anything were to happen to you..." Holmes said softly.

"You can't keep us in hiding any longer, dad. You can't protect us anymore," Edmond said. "It is time for us to help you."

Chapter Twenty-Four

Two months later

"Rebecca," Marguerite called up to her daughter. "We do not want to be late, my dearest."

Two months had passed since the last Boxer murder and the police had dubbed it a cold case. Percy, Holmes, and Edmond were still looking for Moriarty's connection to the murders but had only told Marguerite pieces of the puzzle. But that day, was Rebecca's day. She was to be presented officially at court. Her ball was planned for later that year at Mycroft's estate. Cedric was her official escort as he was not a family member nor was he spoken for. He waited beside Marguerite wringing his white gloves, absentmindedly.

"Thank you for agreeing to do this, Cedric," Marguerite placed a hand on his arm.

"It is a great honor, *madame*," he said. "I am flattered by her request."

"And are you willing to be considered as my daughter's suitor? That will undoubtedly be the consensus tonight," Marguerite asked.

Cedric turned to look at her and straightened.

"*Madame*," he started. "I have always had the highest respect for your daughter. I must confess, though my reputation is somewhat tainted by certain things, I have always had a... vested interest in Rebecca. I cannot tell you when this consideration started, or when it formed into more than a brotherly regard, but rest assured, my regard for her is far from a brother. I intend to discuss the prospect with Mr. Holmes later this evening if that is agreeable with you and her, of course."

Marguerite's smile broadened as she leaned toward him and kissed his cheek.

"I believe I may speak for my husband and myself when I say we are very glad," she said. Cedric sighed in relief but movement at the top of the stairs drew his attention.

Turning his gaze up, his breath caught in his throat. Rebecca stood, radiant in her white gown, at the top of the stairs. He felt Marguerite's eyes on him, but he could not look at her, he could not look at anything apart from the angel floating down the stairs to him. Rebecca's eyes never left his. Finally, Cedric came to his senses to offer his hand as she reached the last three steps.

"Beautiful, *ma Cherie*," Marguerite said.

"Stunning," Cedric agreed.

"Thank you," she blushed. "And thank you, Cedric for being my escort tonight. I am confident in my choice and thank you for accepting."

"The honor is mine, Rebecca," he replied and offered his hand. When she slipped hers into his strong grasp, he raised her fingers to his lips and kissed them. Sliding her hand through his arm, he escorted her down the stairs and into the carriage that had been sent by the queen and made their way to Buckingham Palace.

Rebecca had never had such a wonderful time. Cedric was the perfect companion. He retrieved her refreshments and made sure she was not overly warm. Never had she thought she would be the envy of every woman, but when she entered the ballroom, after the official presentation to Queen Victoria and her son Prince Edward, on Cedric's arm, she instantly felt the stares. Cedric placed a hand over hers as it rested on his forearm and confidently escorted her to her place with the other young ladies.

After the Queen and Prince entered, the music was commanded to begin. All the young ladies were escorted to the dance floor by their young men and the first dance was to begin. Having only had her brothers as male companions while learning a dance, she was eager to begin with Cedric.

"Pray, take your places for the Viennese Waltz," the Harold said. Rebecca swallowed hard.

"Oh no," she whispered. "Could it not have been the regular waltz?"

As she placed her hand on Cedric's shoulder and raised her left hand holding her dress so she would not trip, she gazed up into Cedric's eyes. Leaning down, he whispered in her ear.

"Follow my lead. I will never let you fall."

She felt his hand slip around her waist and his right-hand slide under her left keeping her hand up. Just as the music began he winked at her and began the dance. She felt lighter than air.

Holmes and Marguerite watched as their daughter danced for the third time with Cedric. No other man had caught her eye though many had tried. Marguerite slipped her arm through Sherlock's and looked up at him.

"Well, my dear," Holmes started. "I do believe our daughter's heart has been spoken for."

"If she is anything like me, Sherlock," Marguerite said. "She is halfway in love with him already."

Holmes chuckled and raised her hand to his lips.

"If she is anything like you, *mon coeur*," Holmes said. "He will be the luckiest man on earth."

Marguerite's eyes softened as she gazed up at her husband. "Do you recall our first dance?" He nodded once. "It was in a similar setting to this you danced away with my heart,

Sherlock. I love you."

"I love you, Margot," he whispered kissing her hand. Looking away from his heated gaze, her eyes drifted to the recently knighted Percy dancing with Alexandra.

"And if Percy has his way, he will be married come next spring," Marguerite said.

"I do believe he is already planning for it," Holmes answered.

"*Bon*," she said. "It will be good for him to settle down. Now if we can only find someone for Edmond."

"His heart is still hurting, my love," Holmes responded.

"*Oui*," Marguerite said. "But we can at least begin to look for him."

"Are you a matchmaker now, my dearest?" Holmes asked.

"Hardly," she answered. "But a good mother wants all her children happy."

"You are not a good mother," Holmes said. "You are the best." Raising her hand to his lips once more, he took one step in front of her and offered his hand for the dance.

Chapter

Twenty-Five

Rebecca wished to walk for a little way before climbing back into the carriage. Even though her feet hurt from dancing all night, her heart felt lighter than a cloud.

Her family agreed to walk with them to rid themselves of the stuffiness of the ballroom. Holmes, Marguerite, Watson and Edmond walked together, Percy and Alexandra were a little way ahead and Rebecca and Cedric hung back.

"I want to thank you, Cedric for escorting me today," she said. "I felt at ease with you beside me."

"I am glad of it, Rebecca," he replied. "I would want nothing but your ease when you are with me."

Rebecca looked down and away from him, a blush deepening her cheeks. Cedric took a deep breath and stopped walking for a moment. Rebecca turned to him looking up curiously at his deep blue eyes.

"Forgive me," Cedric said. "I... wanted to speak with you for a moment, if you agree."

"Of course," she replied. "What is it?"

"Rebecca, you are the most intelligent, beautiful,

fascinating, considerate, young woman of my acquaintance. I have seen you grow from a child to this beautiful woman who now stands before. I wish you to know of my intentions and I ask your permission and blessing. I hope to beg an audience with your father tonight to seek his permission to continue our... understanding. If you are agreeable."

Rebecca blinked once unsure if she heard him correctly.

"You are asking to... court me?" She asked for clarification.

"I am," he nodded. "My intentions toward you are honorable but cannot deny the feelings I feel for you. When you were in my arms tonight dancing, nothing has felt more right. And I was jealous of the other men who danced with you."

"You should not have been," she whispered. "I thought only of you."

His chest lightened. "Then do you consent?"

"I do," she answered beaming. "If I am not as excited as I feel, you must forgive me, I did not realize your affection for me extended past brotherly regard."

"Oh my dear, Rebecca," he breathed out. "Believe me when I say, I do not think of you as a sister. Not at all. I should be perfectly honest with you... My intentions do not stop at courting. Do you understand me, Rebecca?"

"You mean marriage?"

"I do."

Rebecca took a deep breath before she bit her lower lip, a move that distracted Cedric and his eyes were pulled to that spot.

"I do not wish to be married just yet," she confided. "I know it is done, but I do not wish to be... a mother yet."

His eyes shot back to hers to see the indecision swimming in her grey depths.

"Nor I a father, yet," he agreed. "There are ways, but I will leave that to your mother to explain." A soft red hue darkened her cheeks.

"Mama has told me some things."

"Good," he gently pulled her chin back to look up at him. "I would never embarrass you, Rebecca. But I find I cannot douse the urge I have to kiss you. Will you let me?"

She nodded slowly and Cedric leaned down. Not trusting himself with more than a soft brush of his lips against hers, it was the hardest moment of his life to pull away. Her eyes were still closed when he looked down at her. She took a deep satisfied breath and opened her glassy eyes.

"I do hope there will be more of that to come," she whispered. "Alexandra was right."

"Right?" he asked.

"Your kiss is most desirable."

Cedric let out an embarrassed chuckle. "I suppose I should not be surprised. Ladies do speak of the oddest things when one is in their confidence. I hope you understand, with her, it was a goodbye and nothing more."

"I do," she answered. "Now this was a hello."

"It was indeed. And there are many more to come." He leaned down slowly again but pulled back when they heard Alexandra's voice.

"Percy, there is something up ahead."

"What is that?" Alexandra asked Percy as they walked together. Percy peered through the fog and saw what she meant.

"It appears to be a mound of something," Percy replied. "Perhaps a rough living in the park. Father, perhaps we should go around another way." Percy called to Holmes.

"What is it?" Holmes called back.

He left Marguerite with Watson and walked on ahead. Percy indicated the mound of clothing ahead of them a few feet.

"Alexandra, go back with your father and Marguerite," Holmes ordered. Alexandra did not hesitate.

"What is it, Holmes?" Watson asked.

"I do not know," Holmes called back. "Edmond," he called to his son.

Edmond made sure his mother and Alexandra were safe. Cedric and Rebecca beside them.

"What is it?" Edmond whispered to his father when he reached him.

"I do not like the look of it," Holmes gripped his swordstick tighter.

"Let me go," Percy suggested.

"No, me," Edmond stopped him. Percy looked back. "Of the two of us, I have more hand to hand experience."

Percy nodded and watched as Edmond went toward the huddled mass on the ground. As Edmond approached he could make out an outline of a figure dressed in evening clothes. The closer Edmond got, the more still the figure appeared to be. Then Edmond saw the blood. Dark pools reflected in the flickering light of the lamppost nearby. The body was on its side, the back toward Edmond. Knowing by the amount of blood, the man was either dead or very near to death, Edmond reached out and pulled the figure toward him. The face was revealed. Edmond did not flinch. The man had three carvings in his face. On his two cheeks were the symbols for *collapse* and *mortality*, and on his forehead was the symbol for the word *traitor*. When he looked past the inscriptions to the face, he studied it for a moment then his blood ran cold.

"Are you absolutely certain?" Percy asked after Edmond had asked for Holmes and his brother to meet him. Edmond nodded. "*Oh, mon dieu.*"

"What do we do?" Edmond asked.

"All we can do," Holmes said. "Call the police and tell him."

"We cannot," Percy protested. "Not tonight. Think of Rebecca."

"If he finds out we knew and did not tell him? What then?" Edmond asked. "I agree our sister's happiness tonight is important, but it is one evening in exchange for the rest of her married life. We must tell him. It is only fair to our dearest friend. He would never forgive us if we did not tell him."

"What are you all talking about?" They heard Cedric approaching them and almost too quickly moved to cover the face of the body. "What is it?"

"Cedric, please. Wait. A man has been killed," Holmes announced. "We need to go for the police. But..."

"Who is it?" Cedric asked.

"Cedric, this is not how we... I am so sorry," Percy said. Cedric's brow furrowed as he looked passed Edmond to a hand that was visible. His entire frame froze and in the dim light of the lamppost they saw him weave a moment as the color drained from his face.

"Edmond," Cedric breathed. "What is that ring on his finger?" Edmond did say anything. "Ed, tell me, please!" Cedric said forcefully.

"It is the Somers' family crest," Edmond replied.

His eyes snapped to his. "Gérard?" he breathed. Edmond closed his eyes and nodded. Cedric rushed forward, but Percy held him back.

"No, Ced, listen to me, you do not want to," Percy said.

"Let me go," he ordered. "I need to see."

"Cedric, please," Percy replied.

"I said, let me go!" Cedric, stronger and larger than Percy, pushed him easily to the side and rushed to the body on the ground. Edmond stood back knowing he could stop him but allowing him the courtesy of mourning. His wail, as he fell to his knees, crushed Edmond's heart. Looking over at his sister, Edmond saw the tears in Rebecca's eyes as she covered her mouth with her gloved hand. Marguerite and Alexandra wrapped their arms around Rebecca. Watson went over to Holmes.

"Perhaps I could—" he started.

"No, Watson," Holmes replied softly. "There is no use. He is cold and stiff. He has been dead for many hours."

Cedric held his brother to him and cried out again. His grief felt by all. Percy locked eyes with Edmond, his best friend and they shared a silent moment. Edmond gripped his brother's forearm in reassurance.

When Cedric finally calmed enough to speak, he looked up at Holmes. "Why?" He pleaded.

"He was in debt to Spooner," Holmes said. "Whoever killed Spooner, must have known of their connection. He was a pawn. I am very sorry, Cedric."

"So because I would not give my brother the money he asked for," Cedric started.

"No, Cedric," Holmes stepped forward. "You will not blame yourself for this, do you understand?"

Cedric looked at Holmes as if in a fog. "Could you send for the police, please? My brother deserves the dignity afforded a nobleman. So much of that has already been stripped. I will not allow more. I will not have his body gawked at by passersby."

"I will go," Watson said and glanced back at Alexandra. "Will you see my daughter home?" He asked Percy. Percy nodded.

"She will stay with us until you come to collect her at Baker Street," Marguerite answered as the ladies walked over. Edmond and Percy shielded Cedric and the corpse from their view.

"Please," Rebecca stepped forward. "Let me to him."

"No, sweetheart," Edmond said. "I will not have that image in your mind." She nodded and lowered her eyes from him, but Edmond wrapped his arms around her.

"Go with your mother, Rebecca," Holmes instructed. "We will be along shortly."

"Cedric," she called. Edmond and Percy parted for a moment allowing Cedric to walk through them and to their sister.

"Forgive me," he said framing her face with his hands. "But what we discussed cannot happen tonight."

"Of course," she confirmed. "I would never ask that. I," she glanced around at her family. Holmes, Percy and Edmond turned their backs giving them a small amount of privacy and Marguerite and Alexandra stepped back. "I am so sorry, Cedric. Please if you... need anything."

"I know," he answered resting his forehead against hers. "This is not how I expected the evening to go."

"Please do not think on it," she replied.

"And I am sorry you saw me so... distraught."

"What? Crying over a loved one? I am pleased you did so. It makes me love you even more," she said. Cedric pulled back and looked at her, his eyes grew wide as a blush crept up her cheeks. "I will leave you in peace. Please do not close yourself off. We are here. I am here, for you." He pulled her to him and crushed his lips to hers in their most provocative kiss yet but she kissed him back with equal fervor. When he pulled back, she smiled up at him and turned, leaving with her mother and Alexandra. Percy walked them to the end of the park and hailed a cab.

"This makes four," Edmond said covering Gérard's face with his coat.

"What is the symbol?" Percy asked when he returned. Cedric sat on a park bench nearby.

"Traitor," Edmond answered. "I should speak with Uncle Mycroft."

"Go, Edmond," his father said. "We will convene at Baker Street in the morning."

Chapter

Twenty-Six

Two weeks later...

"Another murder, read all about it! *Sixth* Boxer Murder, evening paper! Whitehall in panic! Document stolen right from under Downing Street's nose! Get your paper!" The man cried outside the window of 221B Baker Street two weeks after Cedric's brother Gérard was found dead. Though Rebecca had offered their help, they had rarely seen Cedric during that time. Percy stayed over at his flat that evening and found him passed out drunk the next morning, an empty bottle of whisky in his hand. Helping him up to his room and calling for his manservant to help him into the bath and bed, Percy went to Baker Street the next morning, Moriarty the center of conversation.

Now, nine days after the funeral, Cedric sat with them in Baker Street more determined than ever to help them solve this case.

Edmond and Percy sat opposite each other in Holmes' and Watson's old armchairs. Mycroft sat on the chaise lounge, his feet stretched out in front of him, his hands clasped over his stomach in a position of relaxed revelry. His family, however, saw his intensely conscious eyes and behind them a brain that was constantly working.

Holmes puffed on his cigarette and paced in front of the fire.

"Six murders, Sherlock," Mycroft finally spoke. "Six…" he sighed harshly. "These last two had state documents that were stolen and have yet to be recovered! All you can say is, we have to wait?"

"We all know it's Moriarty behind this Uncle, we just do not know what to do about it," Percy explained. Edmond glanced over at his father.

"I understand that, my lad, but it doesn't matter who is behind it, as long as it stops. The Prime Minister is beside himself. We have tried to keep the papers at arm's length but somehow they're finding it all out. Relations with China have never been so strained. Our peace talks with the ambassador have turned into war rallies. Their allies are readying their troops. If we don't get this solved, we just might have a world war on our hands, and you know what that will do to the economy."

"Have you spoken with their leader?" Percy offered.

"He refuses to see our ambassador and sends his son-in-law," Mycroft said. "We have to stop this Boxer frenzy before it tears this country in half."

"Attempt to beg an audience with the Chinese leader himself, once more," Edmond said.

"It is of no use, my boy," Mycroft replied. "He will not see us."

"Tell him," Edmond started. "The tranquility of T'ai Shān is at stake."

"What does that mean?" Percy asked.

Edmond's eyes told him he wasn't going to say.

"We all know who and why. His attack on Cedric the night Rebecca was presented to society was a deliberate and personal attack," Holmes finally said with a glance at Cedric. His grip on the whisky tumbler increased for a moment, but Cedric locked eyes with Holmes.

"He used my brother as a pawn to get to you through me," Cedric summarized.

"I believe so," Holmes answered.

"Gérard never did keep good company," Cedric sighed. "But this? He did not deserve. My father must be rolling over in his grave. Do you have a plan, Mr. Holmes?"

"A formation of one," Holmes began but stopped when they heard Watson's step on the stair. He walked in a moment later with an evening paper.

"Who is it this time, Watson?" Holmes asked.

"Young Sir Robert Forester, youngest son of the Earl of Springfield," Watson explained.

"Read it to us, Doctor," Holmes asked.

Watson took off his hat and as he struggled with his overcoat, Percy stood and helped him.

"How is Miss Watson this evening, Doctor?" Percy asked.

Watson looked over at him. "Though your timing could improve considerably," Watson started. "She is well."

"Forgive me, I was merely interested," Percy said.

"Yes, I know what you're interested in. But this was neither the time nor the place," Watson replied stepping into the center of the room, leaving Percy standing alone with Watson's coat.

"'Sir Robert Forester, youngest son of the Earl of Springfield was found dead yesterday morning. The twenty-eight-year-old was shot through the head; death followed instantaneously. He was found in Soho, well known for its opium dens. He had a curious symbol carved into his forehead around the bullet wound.' There's the symbol printed below," Watson explained as he read. "'Young Forester, who had just returned from a three year journey across Europe, was an aide to his father, who holds a seat in Parliament. It is believed Forester stole vital papers from his father, with the intent to sell them. The papers were not found on his person.'"

"Sherlock, something must be done," Mycroft said.

"You are just as capable as I, Mycroft," Holmes said.

"Dammit man, this is a matter of National Security!" He cried.

"I am not retained by the government!" Holmes yelled. "I have told you my reasoning that is all!"

"If you think—" Mycroft yelled and stood.

Edmond stood between them.

"Please!" Edmond bellowed above his uncle's tone. "This is not the way. Arguing amongst ourselves is not going to help anyone. May I remind you we have six men dead? That's six families who are in mourning. Fathers who have lost sons, uncles who have lost nephews, and brothers who have lost brothers. Let us remember even though this is a matter of National Security, our lives are cheap if we overlook the humanity and go straight for the logic. I, for one, want to stop this, not for England's sake, but for the thousands, millions of families just like those six who will lose their loved ones in a war. Please, listen to each other. Work together. Nothing can stop us then."

Everyone was quiet after Edmond's speech.

"I will go and request a meeting with the Chinese leader," Mycroft finally said.

"I will go and speak with the boy's parents," Holmes began. "Then send out word to my irregulars to keep their ears open for anything pertaining to Moriarty. If he won't come to us, perhaps we will have to seek him out. Edmond, Percy, go to the professor's former residence and see if you can discover anything."

"What about me, sir?" Cedric asked standing.

"I need you here," Holmes said. "With all of us gone, I need to be sure my wife and daughter are safe. Can I leave them in your hands, Cedric?"

"Of course, but would I not be of more value to you out there looking with you?"

"This task is one I would not give to just anyone, Cedric," Holmes said. "I need to make sure they are safe so I can go about my work. I leave them in your charge."

"I will guard them with my life," Cedric vowed.

"I know it," Holmes answered. "We all must be on our guard. We know who we're dealing with. We must be one step ahead, at all times which will be difficult since we're so far behind already. But, I doubt these murders and theft of government documents has anything to do with the Boxers. This is just to entice us to solve it and to get close to him. If anything is amiss, if we feel anything is wrong, we must let the others know. No more going on by yourselves." He looked at Edmond. "We must be together."

Percy and Edmond sat in a rumbling train car watching the English countryside roll past them at unbelievable speed. Percy sat reading while his brother dozed across from him. Chuckling at something in the letter, Percy bit his lower lip hiding his grin as Edmond woke and straightened in his seat.

"Amusing?" Edmond asked him. Percy looked up.

"Yes," he answered, folding the letter and placing it in his inner breast pocket.

"May I ask who it is from?" Edmond asked.

"Miss Watson and I have been communicating," Percy admitted.

"Ah, that explains the good doctor's rather cold attitude towards you," Edmond said.

"I suppose," Percy shrugged. "But my intentions are entirely gentlemanly."

"Of course they are, but Dr. Watson does not know you. Imagine if the places were reversed? Imagine it was a man interested in Rebecca... A man such as you, a man of the world whom you do not know..."

"I believe you and I both would have an issue with that," Percy replied.

"Not to mention Father's reaction," Edmond said.

"What do I do then to prove my intentions?" Percy asked.

"You are asking me?" Edmond laughed. "As if I know? The fair sex is your specialty, brother-mine."

As Holmes and Watson journeyed to the Earl of Springfield's estate just outside of London, Watson could hold in his query no longer.

"Holmes," he began. "Why have you been so casual

about this whole affair? I mean, a serial killer with six victims? I would have thought this would be fascinating to you." Watson said.

"There are interesting aspects, I agree," Holmes replied.

"What aren't you telling me?" Watson asked his old friend. Holmes did not look at him. "After all we've been through, I would have hoped you would trust me enough and know I would never reveal anything you would not want the public to know. I believe I have proven that to you. The Balthazar case? The Irish Conundrum? The Johannes Waltz? Those among many others have never seen the light of day because you requested I not publish them. So, I ask you, if you ever cared for me as a friend, as you professed to have, tell me what is bothering you. Can I help you? It seems this is something that is hindering you. Would it not help if I knew it too and carried the burden with you?" Watson asked earnestly.

"It is not that I do not trust you, Watson," Holmes said not looking at him. "I... have my reasons."

"No, Holmes, no, no more of that. You need to tell me the truth. I think I deserve that much," Watson said.

"It is not mine to tell," Holmes stared out the window.

"Then whose?" Watson asked. Holmes said nothing. "Marguerite's? Percy's? Edmond's?" Watson proceeded. When Holmes said nothing, Watson read the truth in his tense jaw. It was something to do with his family. "You can tell me anything, my dear friend. I believe you would tell me something if it was Percy considering he is courting my daughter, but Marguerite? Perhaps not. You do not think I would see her any differently, do you? Dear god, that woman is a wonder, nothing could ever make me see her differently..." he stopped for a moment. "Was there an absolute reason you *had* to marry her? It wouldn't be the first case and it most certainly wouldn't be the last. If you, perhaps..."

Holmes slowly turned to his friend a contemplative scowl lining his face.

"I fell in love with the lady, what are you asking me?" Holmes asked.

"Nothing, I am just trying to understand why you would not wish to tell me. If it is something to do with

Marguerite and perhaps something society deems... unnatural, I could understand why you wouldn't wish to tell me, but know this Holmes I would never look upon her any differently." When he said nothing again, Watson decided to ask it plainly. "Was Percy perhaps... conceived..." Watson didn't know how to say it.

"On our wedding night," Holmes finished. "What do you take me for? A blackguard?" His tone was harsh.

"I am sorry, I am merely trying to understand," he said. "What scandal could possibly—"

"Scandal?" Holmes asked surprised. "You think there is a scandal surrounding this?"

"Well, I-I," Watson stuttered.

"Perhaps, my dear doctor, I kept them a secret for the same reason you kept Alexandra a secret for all those years. Perhaps I didn't want them used against me? Perhaps I didn't want the uncertainty of my profession to affect them. Perhaps I wanted to keep them safe from—" Holmes stopped himself.

"Safe from whom?" Watson coaxed.

Holmes closed his eyes and breathed deeply. "Her father," he said.

Chapter
Twenty-Seven

Percy and Edmond stood outside staring at the ancestral home of the Moriarty family. They had only heard stories about the majestic domicile and even those stories could not prepare them for the ancient beauty that stood on the moor.

The place was deserted, apart from the overabundance of grouse crying around them. The fog rolling in off the Dales rendered the abandoned manor a queer and unsettling atmosphere.

"Well," Percy sighed. "No use in standing out here. Let's go in."

They made their way across the graveled drive and forced the door open. They stood in the grand entryway seeing the cobwebs and dust that covered every item in the room. A cold chill ran down Percy's back as he looked around. Furniture still half covered with white sheets, surrounded them and the chandelier was still wrapped in moth eaten cloth. The grand staircase, once the gem of the entire county of Yorkshire was now rotted, tarnished, and covered in dust. The walls were discolored and yellowing while the furniture that had not been covered, still held the secret brilliance of an age gone by. There were roses in a vase on the side table, shriveled and dehydrated; they reflected the death and decay around them. Edmond eyed the room and again the book; *Great Expectations*, came to his mind. Then he shuddered remembering Miss White and his tea engagement with her and her sister a month ago. He was surprised he made it out of there alive. But he would rather be back there than in this menacing manor holding on to the memories his parents had told him.

The brothers walked through the entry and to the ballroom. As soon as they entered, they stopped in awe. The twenty-foot ceiling with gold gilded accents echoed the splendor of old. The web covered chandelier hung in the center of the room and the orchestra gallery loomed high above them in the opposite direction.

"Percy," Edmond called to him when his brother had not moved from the doorway. "We have a job to do."

"Yes, I know," he answered. "But just think, this is where it all started. This is where they met. They danced together on this floor. They fell in love under that chandelier. All those hopes and dreams shattered by him... it makes me angry to think of the life they could have had without him."

"Don't think on it, come," Edmond coaxed.

A large fireplace stood in the wall to their left. The brothers looked at each other and headed in that direction. Edmond stripped off his coat and rolled up his shirt sleeve. He looked at Percy who nodded. Edmond reached in. Blindly groping for what their father said would be there, Edmond extended his arm up into the chimney. He felt something but knew instantly that was not what he was looking for. A chill ran down his back, he hated rats. Finally, his fingers touched the lever. He yanked on it and the wall to their right popped opened. Edmond smiled in triumph and pulled back. Dusting off his arm, he pulled on his coat. Percy went to the door and yanked it back a little further. The secret chamber Holmes had said would be there, was musty and smelled of old moth eaten books and documents.

"One of us stays out here while the other goes inside," Percy said.

Edmond looked at his brother sarcastically. "A brilliant idea, my dear Watson," he answered.

Not dignifying an answer, Percy went on, "This just feels wrong... considering."

"Don't think about that," Edmond replied as he headed in. Two minutes passed before he came back out with a portfolio.

"What did you find?" Percy asked.

"You'll have to be the judge," Edmond answered and opened the portfolio. "Look here."

"'We the undersigned do solemnly swear that whatever is contained herein will not, upon penalty of death be revealed.' Yes, I believe it is it. Well done!" Percy cheered clapping his brother on the shoulder.

"Well done indeed," A voice from the orchestra gallery purred.

Percy's grip on his walking stick intensified. Edmond's body took a stance like a cheetah ready to pounce. It was a gentle, quiet voice but it held darkness and it was that darkness both brothers had heard.

"I must congratulate you both," the sly, snake like voice continued from the darkened balcony. "Only one other person knew of my secret hiding place. I must say, I've enjoyed watching you both."

"Who are you?" Percy called.

"Come now," the voice continued. "Surely you know... And by the way, Percy, your sword stick would do little good," they both heard the click of a revolver being cocked. "Now, Edmond on the other hand I'm sure could dodge but... I'd rather not find out... yet."

"Show yourself, you monster," Edmond called.

"Tsk, tsk, tsk, dear me, just as impatient as your father." There was movement in the gallery as a single match was lit and illuminated a face for a brief moment before it was lowered to light a pipe. "Murray, Jameson, turn up the gas."

Percy partially pulled out his sword from his walking stick. Edmond's hand on his arm stopped him. Someone moved near the door and the light increased.

"Ah," the voice continued. Edmond and Percy heard slow footsteps on the winding staircase leading up to the gallery. "That's better."

They couldn't see him yet. He was slowly making his way down the stairs but kept his face hidden.

"You know I must confess, I could have killed you both about fifteen times since you broke in here... which is a crime by the way, breaking and entering and robbing me. But I have to say, I enjoyed your little repartee and at my time of life amusement comes very infrequently. It reminded me of the time I caught your father and his dimwitted brother Mycroft attempting to do the same thing," the tone of his voice increased, then immediately lessened back to the purr it was before.

"They were about your age; Sherlock was a couple of years younger probably. But the similarity in both cases is... striking," he let the s's linger like a snake hissing its tongue. "But of course, nothing quite compares to the time I heard Holmes and your mother in here making plans to run away together. I admit my temper has mellowed with age," again his voice crescendoed and then lowered. The drastic tone difference shook them both to the core but they stood tall and showed no fear. "And instead of shooting you as I did your father, I will simply say... Welcome, it's good to finally meet you both," the man turned with a sickening grin on his face full into the light as he reached the final step. A massive scar stretched from the top of his forehead, over his left eye and down to his lip.

"Moriarty," Percy breathed.

"Coward," Edmond said.

"Come now, is that any way to greet your grandfather?" Moriarty asked.

Chapter Twenty-Eight

"You *married* the daughter of *Professor* James *Moriarty?*" Watson shrieked.

"Keep your voice *down*," Holmes urged, his tone low and intense.

"You *married* the daughter of your arch enemy," Watson stated.

"I'm aware of that fact, Watson," Holmes said sarcastically.

"How? I-I mean... did you *know?*" Watson asked shocked.

With a heavy sigh, Holmes began, "Moriarty was a professor at my university. He was one of my favorite tutors. I had not met a mind equal to my own until I met him. I do believe that is what drew my fascination to him. Mycroft and I enjoyed his company both in class and socially," Holmes began explaining.

"Mycroft? Your brother went to University at the same time as you, but surely the difference in your ages—" Watson started.

"Our parents were dead," Holmes shrugged. "Mycroft took care of me. He moved from our family estate to a cottage just off the university campus. As distrusting as he is of people, when Moriarty took a personal liking to me, Mycroft wanted to know why. He would join me at our tutorials. And oh, Watson, the talks we had, the three of us... We three began a strong friendship. Moriarty invited us to dinners at his ancestral estate in Yorkshire. It was there I met Marguerite, his daughter. Her mother, a French woman, had died many years ago. It is unclear if she and Moriarty were ever married. She was living as a woman of the evening when she died. Marguerite, not wanting to fall into the same profession as her mother, went to her father as a last resort. He had left her mother when she was a very young child.

"I was nineteen; she was seventeen when we met. Moriarty was watching us and I believe he was attempting to groom me to take his place as head of his organization. But I noticed I was a different man when I was with her. Marguerite brought out a human element in me, when I did not know how to be human. I didn't realize how solitary and lonely a calculating mind could be until she danced into my life. As I continued to engage with her, I realized my judgment of women, tainted by my own past with my mother, was biased. Her shrewd judge of character was only surpassed by her beauty. And on more than one occasion I found myself baffled by her assumptions.

"During my time at University, there was a particularly brutal murder of a professor and all eyes turned to Moriarty, as he and the gentleman never saw eye to eye. I approached the case with the express purpose of proving him innocent. What I found was, he was not only guilty of that crime, but several others. He was running a league of criminals from his lodgings at University. It was already a large and lucrative business when Mycroft and I discovered it.

"The Home Office utilized our findings to build a case against him, but he was too clever for them. He had intended the murder to be so obvious people would believe he was framed, in order to take the attention off of his other dealings. We went to the police with the evidence we had garnered.

"When that evidence was mysteriously misplaced, Mycroft and I attempted to burgle his house looking for the book in which he recorded all of his dealings. Marguerite caught us breaking into Moriarty's secret vault. After revealing who we were, her love for me dissuaded her from raising the alarm. She could not believe the father she loved could be a mastermind and a killer, but my evidence was too strong and she saw it was true.

"We had been meeting secretly for a time and on the eve of his arrest, I begged her to come away with me. When she eventually agreed, Moriarty revealed he had been listening to us the entire time above in the gallery. He disowned his daughter, called her a whore like her mother, and told me my curse would be I would know he was alive and well and every time I had an intense feeling as if he was watching me, he would be or while on a case I could not solve or lay my finger on the culprit, it would be him. He swore to me if I were to be with Marguerite, he would find her and use her against me. He would kill her in front of me and I would be powerless to stop him. That was his curse for us.

"The last thing I remember, he raised his gun, I pushed Marguerite behind me as he aimed and fired. I awoke in a hospital a few days later. Marguerite and Mycroft were there. They told me Moriarty had disappeared and no one knew where he was. I knew then that when Marguerite and I did marry I would have to keep her a secret. I would have to hide her. I could never let her suffer and die for my own cause. I did try to make her see reason by telling her I could not marry her, but she is a fierce woman and she told me I was an imbecile and that we were getting married whether I agreed or not," Holmes chuckled. "We did marry, in secret, Mycroft was our only witness. Moving to her homeland of France seemed like a logical idea and I bought a house by the sea. My mother had left me some money and I used it to make my bride happy. When we had Percy, our life was complete.

"But then I got news London was being terrorized by a serial killer and thief of Parliamentary papers. He left the calling card; JM carved into each of the victim's foreheads. It was a ploy to get me back to London, of course. Marguerite was seven months into carrying Edmond at the time. I waited until after he was born to go over to London. I thought I could find the professor and have him arrested, then return to my wife and sons. Alas, he proved good to his curse, and was elusive. I returned to Marguerite several months later and stayed with her for eight more years, traveling to England very rarely. Five years after we had Edmond, Rebecca was born and I had no desire to go back to London.

"But then another case drew me back to this grand old city. This time I met with the Professor face-to-face. He had found my lodgings with Mycroft. He told me he knew where Marguerite was and where my children were. He knew names, ages, and even what they looked like. He swore if I went back to them, he would kill them all. I hurried back to Marguerite never feeling so sick. After a long conversation, we agreed for the children's sake I had to make it appear I followed his instructions and returned to London. I set up with my brother. That was the summer of 1880, that next year-"

"We met," Watson provided. Holmes nodded.

"Then I had the perfect idea, partner with you and encourage you – through my own reverse method – to write up our cases. Providing Moriarty with the evidence he needed, proving I had indeed stayed in London. You were always so good as to never publish anything regarding my recurrent absences but I'm certain he knew. True to his curse, my career has been to hunt down my former friend, mentor and my father-in-law to bring him to justice. He eluded me for a long time. Then in May of ninety-one, as I'm sure you recall, I met up with him one last time.

"My children were nearly grown and I had missed so much. I was tired of living in the shadow of fear. I made sure it was a place Moriarty would recognize. The Falls of Reichenbach was where he first met Marguerite's mother. I intended to end the life of Professor Moriarty," Holmes paused for a moment. "Do you recall the letter I wrote to you that day?" Holmes asked. Watson nodded. "Do you recall the first few lines?"

"You know I have the entire thing memorized, Holmes. 'I write these few lines through the courtesy of Mr. Moriarty, who awaits my convenience for the final discussion of those questions which lie between us.'" Watson quoted.

Holmes nodded.

"My wording was deliberate. I couldn't tell you he and I were going to fight over his daughter, my wife and my children. Those questions which lay between us were questions regarding my family," he said. "When I met him, he uttered some of the most disgusting things I had ever heard. It made me angry. I lunged for him and we fought. I was stronger and more agile and, perhaps, more passionate. I knew if only I could end his life right then, he would never be able to hurt Marguerite. I was going to go to you, when I saw you at the falls. I was going to tell you everything and even invite you to join me and meet them. But then I saw Moran... I knew what I had to do. Moran knew about Marguerite, as well. I had to get to her. I had to make sure Mycroft would put an end to the body of the snake whose head I had just cut off.

"When I came back those three years later, I was going to tell you again, but then realized it was not over. My children's lives were at stake. I was their father. I had to protect them, even if it meant not being part of their lives for many, many years. As you know, we would communicate daily, with those letters you were always so curious about. I would visit them when I could. I hoped now all was safe... but it appears his curse is still upon me. Moriarty has returned," Holmes sighed and was silent for a moment.

"I am truly sorry for never having told you," he went on. "But I hope you can forgive me and understand, as a father, why I did what I did," Holmes looked over at his friend. Watson sat staring at him listening to every word.

"Holmes, always forgiven," Watson said.

The corner of Holmes' lip tipped up.

"Thank you, my dear friend. But I am sure you've heard enough of my voice for now. We have arrived at Sir Robert's parents' house." Holmes said.

"Sir Robert?" Watson blinked. "Oh," he gasped remembering. "Right, the case... yes, the Boxer murderer, or Moriarty... sorry, I was not thinking of that."

"Clearly, my old friend," he replied gently. "We have

some questions for them. We must fulfill our portion of the arrangement with Mycroft and my sons. I know I have given you a lot to comprehend, Watson. Let us get back to the case at hand. The rest of the story will keep. Right now, the game is a foot once more and 'on this charge cry *god for Harry, England and St. George.'"

Watson chuckled as the carriage came to a stop and they filed out.

Chapter
Twenty-Nine

Percy and Edmond were led to the one usable room in the house. The private dining hall of Moriarty's estate was just as elegant and dingy as the rest of the house. Seated at the table by Moriarty's men, Percy and Edmond assessed their situation. The outlook was grim.

"Now, I hope you both enjoy grouse," Moriarty said taking his fork and knife in his hands. Jameson, one of his men, took the warming lid off his plate. A large roasted grouse lay on a bed of sauce. "Well done," he beamed up at him proudly. "Please eat," he indicated the plates in front of them. Percy and Edmond looked at each other and Percy nodded once. They took the warming lid off their own plates to reveal the same meal. Murray, Moriarty's other confederate, opened a bottle of wine and poured a little in each of their glasses.

Moriarty bit into his meal with rabid ferocity. Percy and Edmond did not eat, only moved the food around on their plates to make it look like they were eating.

"It is so nice to be able to have a meal with my grandsons. Tell me, Percy, is there any special lady in your life?" Moriarty asked.

"No," he answered looking directly at him.

"Come, come, come, a strapping young man like you? No female? I'm sure you have had multiple, just none strike your fancy... hmm?" He chuckled. "With that accent of yours you probably have them all eating out of your hand," Moriarty said. "What about you, Edmond?"

"That is not something I am interested in," Edmond replied.

"Oh dear god, you're not, are you? You're not one of those..." Moriarty said.

"No, I am not, I am just not interested in a relationship at this time," Edmond replied.

"Oh good, had me worried," he answered.

"Why are we here?" Percy asked.

"You tell me, you entered my home. I merely extended the invitation to my grandsons to have dinner with me. And don't think I haven't noticed you haven't eaten anything. Afraid it's poisoned? Why would I poison you when I could have shot you earlier?" Moriarty asked.

"Well," Edmond started. "If it is merely an invitation, we can leave at any time," he stood to go. Before he got to the door, Murray stepped in front of it and Edmond heard the click of a revolver. He could have taken Murray down in a single strike, but when he turned, the gun was pointed at Percy. Edmond knew, had it only been him, he would have been able to clear the room, but with Percy there, Moriarty would use his brother against him and that was something he would never allow.

"Actually," Moriarty said, the revolver was in his hand, resting the butt of the gun on the table. "It wasn't just an invitation. Sit down, Edmond. I haven't finished my meal. It's very rude to leave before the host has finished his meal."

Edmond locked eyes with his brother who was still seated at the table.

"I merely thought a nice meal beside a roaring fire would be much better than a cold, dark, cell," Moriarty said. "But if you would prefer it, that can be arranged."

"Our father knows we are here," Percy said as Edmond

sat down.

"Of course, but he also received a note from you saying the weather took a turn and you decided to stay overnight. Now it's up to you whether you stay in the dungeon or you stay in the comfortable rooms upstairs."

"Thank you... grandfather," Percy said. "We appreciate your hospitality." Looking over at Edmond, he implored him to play along. Percy cut into his fowl and began to eat.

"Forgive us for bursting in on your grief, my lord," Holmes addressed the Earl of Springfield.

"Not at all, Mr. Holmes," he answered offering them seats. "My wife is not well. I beg you to excuse her for not receiving you."

"Quite so, my lord, our condolences on your loss," Holmes replied.

"Thank you," the earl answered. His dark black suit and the black strip of cloth banded around his upper arm were the only outward expressions of mourning.

"If I may ask you some questions, my lord," Holmes treaded gently as he sat beside Watson on the settee. The earl nodded.

"Of course," he replied.

"Thank you. Was it usual for your son to be on that side of town at that time of night?"

"Quite unusual, in fact. I know of no reason why he would be there, in that place... he knew no one there," the earl answered. "He was always such a good man."

"Perhaps a friend from university convinced him to go?" Watson offered.

"He never did finish Oxford. He went traveling with his uncle, my wife's brother when he finished secondary school. He had only been home a few months when he left again to travel Europe. When he came back, he and my other son Rufus had a falling out. No one knew why. He left quite suddenly and did not attend his brother's wedding six years ago. When he came back from his travels four years ago, he and his brother began speaking again. Robert became my secretary and would have been his brother's when Rufus takes over for me..." the earl's voice cracked and he cleared his throat attempting to hide the emotions that overcame him. When he could not, he stood and went to pour himself a drink. "Forgive me," he said and took a drink. "I tell you, Mr. Holmes, my son was a good man and for anyone to wish him harm is unconscionable."

"Yet someone did wish him harm, my lord, someone killed him," Holmes said matter-of-factly. Watson gently cleared his throat. Holmes looked over at him and continued. "Of course, he must have been a good man," he clarified and looked to Watson who nodded slightly. "I do wish to find whoever did this and bring some peace to you and Lady Forester."

"Thank you, Mr. Holmes," he said.

"Now you say you have an elder son?" Holmes asked.

"Yes, Lord Rufus," the earl said.

"What age is he?" Holmes asked.

"Eight and thirty," The earl replied.

"And he is married?" Watson asked.

"He is, six years ago, to the second daughter of Lord Paynetree," he answered.

"She is much younger than he, I perceive," Holmes replied.

"What does that have to do with anything?" The earl asked.

"Simply to establish the facts, it is my way," Holmes said. "Do they have any children?"

"One son, Howard, he's only three," the earl answered.

Holmes nodded slightly. "Might I speak to your son?"

"I'm afraid he left last night. He wanted his wife to hear this terrible news from him, not the local newspaper boy," he explained. "He should be home. I shall get you his address."

"I appreciate it, my lord," Holmes said.

"Of course," he replied and handed Holmes his son's card.

"Thank you and thank you for your time. Again, our deepest condolences to you and Lady Forester," Holmes said standing and accepting the card.

"Thank you... I read Mr. Holmes you have a son," he said seeing him to the door.

"Two," he answered.

"Then you know the bond between a father and a son. Find the man who killed him. I am requesting your services. Money means nothing to me, Mr. Holmes. But I beg you, to tell me who he is before you go to the police."

"I cannot promise that, my lord, it is not how I work," Holmes replied. "As a father I know what it is you are asking me, but as a detective I cannot condone that sort of behavior. I promise to do all I can to find this man, but I do not promise to let you know before the police have him in tow. In my experience, my lord, you may need to prepare yourself for the unexpected. Good day to you."

Leaving the house and hailing a cab, the crisp evening air surrounded Watson and Holmes.

"Holmes, what did you mean just now? Why did you tell his lordship to prepare himself for the unexpected? What do you know?" Watson asked as a cab drew up to collect them. Holmes gave the cabbie the address and fell into the seat beside Watson.

"I need more data, Watson," he said. "But I have a train of thought that makes rational sense."

"Oh lord and we all know how you love things that make rational sense," Watson teased. "Can't you tell me anything?"

"I can tell you to look at the eyes of Lady Rufus Forester and see what you see as a medical man," he explained. "Then look at the portrait of her husband."

"Holmes," Watson complained. "You're being cryptic again."

Holmes chuckled. "Forgive me, old chap, just remember this; a man in his mid-thirties and a young woman in her early twenties form an understanding. Enter a man in his mid-twenties, young, full of life, adventurous... come now, Watson you're a father of a young woman, what do you think I mean?"

"You don't think..." he breathed.

"It is possible," he replied. "Where's the best place to hide a jewel?"

"In the midst of other jewels," Watson said.

"And where's the best place to hide a murder?" Holmes asked.

"In the midst of other murders," Watson replied.

"There is so much more to this story than meets the eye," Holmes answered.

"Clearly," Watson said.

"And isn't it just like Moriarty to use a man's hatred for his brother to further his own ambitions?" Holmes asked.

"But for a man to form an attachment with his brother's wife?" Watson said.

"Oh Watson, so delicate," Holmes replied.

Watson cleared his throat. "How are you going to proceed? You don't want him to know you know."

"I doubt very much he is home," Holmes replied.

"But surely, his father said he left last night to be with his wife," Watson said.

"I have no doubt that is what Lord Rufus told his father, but I doubt he ever went home," Holmes answered. "No, wherever he is, I will make a bet with you, he is with the professor."

The cab came to a stop, they got out and headed towards the house.

"Mr. Holmes, sir!" A man behind called. Holmes turned as one of his irregulars rushed up to him. "Sorry, sir, a telegram for you. Mrs. Holmes said it was very urgent and told me you might be here," he explained.

"Thank you, Phillips," Holmes took the telegram.

"How did she know where we are?" Watson asked.

Holmes did not answer. "It's a telegram from Percy and Edmond," Holmes read it. "The weather's taken a turn and they're staying... Watson, get back in that cab, now."

"Why? Where are we going?" Watson asked as Holmes pushed him back.

"Victoria Station, as fast as you can," Holmes yelled to the cabbie.

"Whatever for?" Watson asked.

"My sons are in danger," Holmes said, his fingers curling around the telegram.

Chapter Thirty

Later in the evening, Edmond and Percy had been forced to retire. However drab and austere their lodgings were, it was a sigh of relief not to be imprisoned in the dungeon. Edmond was at the window attempting to see if he could squeeze out of it and scale the wall. Unfortunately, the windows were designed to be mere arrow slits from the middle ages and would not permit a human body, and certainly not one as well defined and broad as Edmond's to fit through. There was a knock at Edmond's door. Percy walked in, closing the door quickly behind him.

"Any luck in your room?" Edmond asked.

"None, the windows are the same as yours," Percy said. He sat on the side of Edmond's bed in a huff.

Edmond walked over from the window and sat beside his brother. "I heard Jameson and Murray are going to take turns guarding the main entrance."

"A nice little pickle we're in," Percy said.

"I could take both of them, easily, if I were alone," Edmond replied.

"You are concerned he would shoot me if you did," Percy said. Edmond nodded. "I *am* familiar with fighting, Ed you don't have the corner market on that," Percy said.

"Sword play is not the same as dodging bullets," Edmond replied.

"Well then, what if I stay in here with the door locked while you go down and kill them? Then come back and get me?" Percy offered.

"I would not kill them," Edmond said.

"Why not? They would kill you," Percy replied.

"Granted, but killing is never a great option," Edmond said. "It is only if necessity permits."

"Oh, how I hate when you go all Chinese proverb on me. You know I have no understanding of that gibberish," Percy said.

Edmond chuckled. "You sound like our uncle. Father will receive our note from Moriarty, I'm sure he didn't use the phrase Father is expecting. He will know something is wrong," Edmond said.

"I wish to heaven I could go into that room and run this sword through him," Percy said.

"Patience," Edmond soothed. "Even if he escapes us here, we are bound to find him later. Our fates are intertwined. Besides, he's gone mad, didn't you notice? That scar was a souvenir from Reichenbach. I believe he has gone insane. Why else would he not kill us on sight? The Moriarty Father knows, did die at Reichenbach. This Moriarty is completely different."

"I did notice," Percy answered. "Why would he threaten us, and then have us to dinner and let us stay in a comfortable room... well," he looked around. "As comfortable as can be expected, instead of the dungeon? We are not in medieval times, but to me, I would have had him on the rack by now if our places were reversed."

"More of your medieval justice, Percy?" Edmond questioned.

"All I am saying is, I know you have a respect your ancestors view, but he is one I have no intention of respecting," Percy said.

"Let me tell you something," Edmond whispered and

leaned over. "I've already thought of about a thousand ways to kill him. I may have the desire to follow the ways of the Orient but when it comes to Moriarty, I become the hot-blooded Frenchman who will kill."

"Never thought I would hear that from you," Percy chuckled. "I am proud of you."

Edmond shook his head and nudged his brother. "Try and get some sleep. Tomorrow we'll start afresh."

That next morning, Edmond woke at seven o'clock which was much later than his daily routine. Unsure as to why, he assessed his body. Since he did not eat or drink anything, he could find no answer as to why he felt sluggish. Slipping out of bed, he was still fully dressed and cautiously went to the door. As silently as he could, he pulled it open. It creaked.

Edmond froze and listened intently.

There was no response. He opened it a little more, enough for him to slip out, and crept down the hall to peer over the banister. There was no sign of Jameson or Murray. Edmond quickly went to his brother's room. He tried the door but Percy had locked it. Noiselessly, Edmond picked the lock and opened the door. Percy was still asleep.

Edmond crept over to his brother and covered his mouth so he would make no sound when he woke. Percy opened his eyes with a start, but seeing his brother, he calmed and nodded.

"I don't see anyone downstairs," Edmond whispered. "We could try and run."

Percy nodded, stood and pulled on his clothes from the day before. They both crept to his door. It opened soundlessly. They got out to the hallway and walked down the stairwell.

The front door was in sight and Moriarty's men were not. Rushing to the door, they opened it and ran. Running so fast down the hill, they didn't watch where they were going and collided with two men walking up. Edmond nearly tackled the man he ran into thinking it was one of Moriarty's men.

"Edmond, Percy, and what in god's name are you two

doing?" The voice was their father's and Edmond stopped himself.

"Moriarty," was all they had to say.

Holmes and Watson took off running toward the house, their guns in hand. Edmond wanted to go after them but Percy stopped him.

"They would be more capable without us," he said.

It was a little over twenty minutes later when Holmes and Watson returned outside.

"There's no sign of him," Watson said.

"Except the obvious ones of remnants of a fire in his room, a bed that's been slept in and clothes in the wardrobe," Holmes replied.

"He was there, sir," Percy said. "He was there, and he held us against our will. I don't know where he is now, but he was there."

"I believe you," Holmes replied. "When I received the note and there was no mention of our home in France, I knew something was wrong. Watson and I got the first train possible. We arrived just an hour ago."

"Moriarty sent the note," Edmond answered.

"So I gathered," Holmes replied. "Now, you're all right, let's get you to the inn. Do you have any change of clothes?"

Percy shook his head. "We were not intending to stay the night."

"When the train did not leave for a half hour, we sent a note to your mother, she and your uncle retrieved some clothes for you both," Holmes handed his son the bag he had left on the ground when he had run inside.

"It was maddening to him not being able to get to you," Watson said. "I had to stop him from starting to walk to Yorkshire on several occasions."

"Train is faster," Percy grinned.

"Let's get you to the inn," Holmes said again. "A hot breakfast and some relaxation are in order. You can then regale us with your adventures."

"What about Moriarty?" Edmond asked.

"All in due time," Holmes replied. They turned and headed down the hill. Holmes did not want to tell his sons he would rather suffer death ten times over than to have them meet with Moriarty again. Watson glanced at him and nodded slightly. Grateful his friend understood him, Holmes led them all to the inn.

Chapter
Thirty-One

Two hours later, feeling refreshed, and dressed in the clothes Holmes had brought, Percy and Edmond sat at a table with Holmes and Watson waiting for their breakfast. Their tea was piping hot and Percy gratefully sipped the beverage. Holmes' eyes passed over his two sons making sure they were well. Even Watson did a once over for his friend's sanity and nodded at him when Holmes' eyes alighted on him.

Eventually the inn's landlady brought them their specially ordered breakfast. Fully conscious his father was watching him, Edmond began to eat.

Percy spoke and relayed the entire story of what happened after they arrived.

"So it's true," Watson said. "Moriarty is alive."

"Obviously," Holmes replied. "What I'm interested in is his changed and somewhat erratic behavior. He had a scar you said, Percy?"

Percy nodded, his mouth full.

"It went from the top of his left forehead, down his left eye and ended on the top of his lip," Edmond described and indicated the devastating wound on himself. Holmes looked over at Watson for his input.

"Yes, a major trauma, likely to produce any number of psychotic behaviors," Watson explained. Holmes nodded. "Do you have any idea where he might be now?" Watson asked.

"No, we did not even know he was going to be gone when we woke up," Percy replied.

Edmond and Holmes locked eyes as if reading each other's minds.

"We have him on the run. He knows we are after him and he just made his last mistake," Holmes said.

"And like a wounded animal, he's at his most ferocious," Edmond continued.

"What mistake?" Percy asked.

"The symbols he carved into the men were more than just the symbol for balance and the words death, traitor, collapse, mortality, and the last one, overthrow," Edmond said.

"What do they mean?" Watson asked.

Edmond's eyes never left his father's.

"We will discuss that at a later time," Holmes replied. "But now if you both have finished your meal, let us return to London. Watson and I have something to follow up on, and I'm sure your uncle needs you," he looked over at Edmond.

As usual, Holmes was right. They all stepped off the train onto the Victoria Station platform to be greeted by Mycroft and Marguerite. Watson watched the looks between his dear friend and his wife. The look in Holmes' eyes when he looked at his wife could only be described as a warning. He told her everything in that one look.

After that brief moment between them, Marguerite's eyes were on her sons. She went to her eldest first and then to Edmond, who embraced his mother and whispered something in her ear.

She nodded but was much paler when she pulled away from him. In a silent gesture of affection and the need for her husband's comfort, Marguerite went to Holmes and took his hand in hers. Other than his face softening as he felt his wife's hand slip into his, Holmes did not react as he stood speaking with his brother.

"I had an interview with the Chinese leader thanks to Edmond's phrase. But when I met with the old man, he knew it wasn't me who knew that phrase and refused to speak to me. He had his interpreter see me out and told me to come back with the man who gave me that phrase. I need Edmond. Is he able to accompany me?" Mycroft explained to his brother.

"You can ask him yourself. Edmond," Holmes called to his son.

"Sir?" Edmond answered walking over from Percy and Watson.

Watson did nothing for a moment but Percy was well aware of the doctor's scrutiny and looked straight ahead, not making eye contact.

"Percy," Watson began. "I want to tell you, it was wrong of me to jump at you earlier. Alexandra is very fond of you, more so than of any other gentleman of her acquaintance and that worries me. I do not wish to lose her so soon," Watson explained. "I know I can do nothing to stop this, as she is a grown woman who is out in society, but the father in me still wants to protect her and keep her hidden. It was wrong of me to say what I did. I want you to know, Percy, if I had to choose a man for her to care for... well, I am glad it is the son of my old friend."

"I wish you to know, Dr. Watson, my intentions toward your daughter are entirely honorable," Percy said. "I would never wish to cause her pain or any difficulty between you and my father."

"I thank you," Watson said. "And as much as it pains me to say this... you have my permission and blessing to form an attachment with my daughter."

"Thank you," Percy breathed.

"But hear me," Watson stepped closer to him and lowered his voice. "If you break her heart, I will take yours out; son of Sherlock Holmes or not."

"I would expect no less, sir," Percy agreed.

Chapter
Thirty-Two

Mycroft had heard about Percy's and Edmond's ordeal with Moriarty and even though they were his nephews, Mycroft loved Edmond as his own son and he couldn't help but remember that horrible night over twenty-five years ago when he had news Sherlock had been shot by Moriarty. He could not imagine getting the news that history had repeated itself and Edmond had been shot.

Mycroft shook his head clearing his thoughts as he and Edmond walked through the back halls of Parliament. Reaching the door, he knocked. The door was opened by an elegantly clad Chinese man and Edmond bowed instinctually.

"We are here to see Ambassador Geming. He is expecting us," Mycroft said.

The man looked over at Edmond who, in compliance with the custom that had been instilled in him, had his eyes lowered and his head down until he was properly introduced.

"What is your name, please?" He asked.

"Mycroft Holmes and this is my nephew, Edmond Holmes," Mycroft said. Edmond lifted his eyes and bowed slightly.

"Come in, please," the man replied and opened the door wider. Mycroft entered and Edmond followed, his eyes lowered yet again. The man led them to a draped, enclosed area. The man spoke something in his native language and the drapes pulled back. The man and Edmond knelt in a bow with their faces turned to the ground. Mycroft stood between them looking at Edmond hardly surprised but a little cautious.

Both men sat back on their heels, Edmond kept his head down and eyes lowered. The man continued speaking in a foreign language. Edmond bowed once more at some point in the man's speech. Eventually the ambassador seated in the chair behind the open drapes said something in a shaky voice. Edmond bowed once more but when he sat back again, he raised his eyes to the ambassador. It was Edmond's turn to speak. When he did, it was in a language Mycroft had never heard his nephew speak before.

Ambassador Geming looked at Mycroft at a point in Edmond's speech, but did nothing more. Geming said something to his secretary, kneeling beside Edmond. He bowed to Geming, stood and walked out of the room. Edmond said something else and gestured to Mycroft. Ambassador Geming nodded to him and gestured to a chair. Mycroft thanked him silently and sat near to his nephew still sitting back on his heels on the floor.

The man asked a question, Edmond answered then translated to Mycroft.

"He asked me how I know the language, culture, and customs of China. I told him about my eight years there," Edmond explained.

"Could you ask him if he knows or has heard of these Boxer murders?" Mycroft asked him.

Edmond did and listened carefully to the ambassador's reply.

"He states he has heard of the murders, but does not believe any Chinaman has anything to do with it," Edmond replied.

"Neither do we, but is there anything he has noticed that may indicate someone?" Mycroft asked.

Edmond asked and translated the reply.

"He says even the crude messages carved into the men's foreheads show a non-native speaking person," Edmond answered.

"In what way?" Mycroft asked.

"The language is too proper for that of a native speaker," Edmond explained. "Most native speakers would use the slang terms not the proper ones."

"Let him know, I speak on behalf of the British Government, when I say, we hope these murders will not affect the possible truce between our two countries," Mycroft said.

"That all depends on the chauvinism of the British people," Ambassador Geming replied in English causing Mycroft and Edmond to look back at him. "There have been three deaths of my countrymen since this whole affair started. All three were beaten to death in the alleyways of your city. Scotland Yard has done nothing to stop or solve these murders. Your people have killed three innocent men simply because of their nationality. Your newspapers have hanged every one of my countrymen and your government has signed the death warrant. Unless this stops, there will be no talk of peace."

"Perhaps, sir, if it was known you and our Prime Minister were in negotiations, it may produce better feeling towards each other," Mycroft offered.

"Your Prime Minister has not come to see me. I traveled a very long distance to meet with him. I have been given no invitation to meet with him, no courtesy that other foreign dignitaries receive. I have been set up here day and night, without even a welcoming gesture. I firmly believe your government wants only the appearance of negotiations, but no actual negotiations will take place. You would not come to me if this was merely a murder of innocent British men. Something else preys on your mind. What has happened?" He looked at Edmond.

Edmond bowed and answered.

"Some government papers have gone missing," he explained.

"These papers have something to do with our countries?" Geming asked.

"Yes," Edmond answered. "We were able to only retrieve two papers; one, the most vital to our nations' securities, is still missing."

"Why have you come to me?" He asked.

"If you would allow me," Edmond bowed. "I believe it is essential our counties work together. The man responsible for these murders, and in an indirect way, responsible for your countrymen's deaths is profiting from both sides of the war. He is an insane man who will destroy countries to get what he desires."

"Sounds like one of your father's mysteries, Mr. Holmes," Geming said.

Edmond bowed but said another phrase. The old man looked at him with raised eyebrows. He said something to Edmond that Mycroft could not understand. Edmond bowed low, his forehead touching the floor and then turned to his uncle.

"He wishes to speak with me alone," Edmond said.

"Are you comfortable with that?" Mycroft's voice was low.

"Yes, you see he was my master's master," Edmond explained. "I will be fine."

Mycroft left the room and listened at the door. Edmond turned to the old man seated in front of him.

"You are a child of two worlds, my son," Geming spoke in his native language.

"Yes, *sifu*," Edmond replied.

"You chose a good name for yourself," the old man said referring to the phrase Edmond had just spoken.

"It is my Zodiac," Edmond answered.

"And very proper. A Metal Horse's greatest attribute is strength. You explain much about yourself in your name. You are self-reliant and like to solve your problems by yourself. But hear me, my son; its greatest downfall is losing those it loves. You must stay clear of grief or it will consume you," the old man warned.

Edmond bowed. "Thank you, *sifu*."

"You are much younger than you act," Geming said. "A good trait, I see. But I also see grief around your eyes... There was young woman you cared for. I can see it in your eyes."

"Yes," Edmond answered. "But she was married to another."

"Grief is a powerful thing," Geming said. "You must not let it cut you off from the rest of the world."

"She was the only woman I have ever cared for," Edmond said.

"How did she die?" Geming asked.

"She was carrying her husband's child," Edmond replied.

"That is something near to your heart," Geming said observing him. "Your own mother died?"

"Nearly," Edmond corrected.

"I see," Geming said. "Death is just a path everyone must take at one time or another. Do not let it cause you such grief that you never love again."

"Yes, *sifu*," Edmond replied.

"I know it is not an easy thing to do," he stated. "I am not long for this world, my son," Geming went on. Edmond looked up at him, a frown marring his handsome features. "I doubt I will see the end of the war. I hope my country will not suffer whatever the outcome. You spent eight years in my country... did you enjoy it?"

"I did, *sifu*," he answered. "Some of my fondest memories are in your country."

"You spent time with your master and his family on the tranquil mountain?" Geming asked.

"I did," Edmond replied.

"I have spent eight days in your country and none of the memories I have made here, apart from meeting you, son, have been my favorite," he said. Looking down at his hand, he raised it towards Edmond. "I know we have only spent a little time together, but I feel like I know you well from your master's kind words about you. Do you still contact him?"

"I do," Edmond replied. "I just received a letter from him last month."

"And that is where you heard the news of his daughter's death?" Geming asked. Edmond immediately looked down. "It is all right, my son. Lei was a beautiful young woman, a credit to our nation. It is obvious you loved her."

"I did," Edmond said softly. "But it is because of me she is dead."

"Was the child yours?" Geming asked.

"No," he shook his head. "But it was our desire to be together that caused her brother to force her marriage."

"And you were whipped," Geming replied. "I know the story." Edmond did not answer but a ghost of the pain he felt that day on his back caused him to flinch. Changing the subject, Geming took off the ring on his right ring finger. "I see it haunts you even now, but want to give you something. Please accept this gift to remember me by."

"I will need nothing to remember you by," Edmond replied.

"Please," he said reaching for him. Edmond stood and, bowing over the elderly man's hand, accepted the jade ring. "We shall not meet again, my son," he continued. "But our brief meeting has given me such hope. I count myself fortunate to have met you."

"And I you, *sifu*," Edmond answered. "If I may, do not allow the actions of but a few dictate the actions of the many. And know when there are multitudes doing something in error, there are a few, striving to do good. I will not rest until those six men whose murders were blamed on your countrymen are avenged and I will devote every energy to bring the men who killed three of your countrymen to justice."

"I believe you will, my son," he answered. "Go, now, come to me again when I have gone to my ancestors. It will make me glad to know you are there."

Edmond bowed again in front of him then walked back to kneel and bow low. With one final look at Geming, Edmond left the room.

Chapter Thirty-Three

Holmes and Watson were shown into Lord and Lady Rufus Forester's drawing room. As the maid went to announce them, they were alone.

"I wonder if Lady Rufus knows where her husband is," Holmes said.

"You have received enough data then? You truly believe that Lord Rufus is involved?" Watson asked.

"Watson, Percy and Edmond described one of their captors as a tallish man, pointed goatee and mustache, dark black hair, with dark brown eyes," Holmes reminded him.

"Murray, yes I remember," Watson said.

"Look at the painting behind you," Holmes indicated.

Watson turned and looked at the lifelike portrait of a man that matched Percy's and Edmond's description in absolute detail.

"Lord Rufus is Murray?" Watson asked.

"It would appear so," Holmes said.

"But why the different name?" Watson asked.

"I did some research on Lord Forester, Lord Rufus's

father, and discovered that he married an American heiress; a Miss Victoria Murray back in New York City," Holmes replied.

"His mother's maiden name," Watson said. "That would make perfect sense."

"I thought so," Holmes teased.

"Holmes," Watson said after a pause. "I want to apologize for what I said in the cab the other day. It was wrong of me to jump to the wrong conclusion regarding you and Marguerite. I know you are an honorable man and would never have compromised her. It just seemed the only possible reason behind your secrecy. Now I know the truth, I feel a fool. Forgive me."

"Do you think I know you so little, my dear friend?" Holmes asked gently. "You have always seen and heard me say I have a profound suspicion of all women. And while that is true, it is not so with Marguerite. Is it not a fact, I have always said all women have an ulterior motive, one that is dastardly? I said those things as a ruse so you would write of me as a confirmed bachelor and Moriarty would never know the truth. You were my alibi, Watson. Without you writing those stories, Moriarty would never have had anything to read and know I was fulfilling my part of the bargain he forced me to accept, and he would continue to leave my family alone.

"I must tell you when you told me about Alexandra in the first few months of our partnership, I heartily thought about telling you. You must understand, I did not know you well enough at that time to tell you, and when I did know you well enough, I thought it was too late."

"It's just... I'm a little... well, now I know how you felt when all my attention was on my wife and daughter. Things have changed even if I did not want them to."

"Oh come now, Watson," Holmes chuckled. "Do not tell me you are jealous," Holmes said even though he knew the answer already.

"Well, no, of course not," Watson stammered.

"Quite so, my dear fellow but there is no need to discuss this further. I believe I hear her ladyship coming our way. Remember what I said, look at her eyes."

The door opened and the loveliest woman Watson had

ever seen entered.

"Forgive me for keeping you waiting, gentlemen," she said. "I am Lady Rufus Forester."

"Good morning, my lady," Holmes started. "I am Sherlock Holmes and this is my friend and colleague Dr. Watson. Forgive us for intruding on your grief. We have been retained by the police to look into the death of your brother-in-law."

Watson looked at her and noticed bloodshot rimmed eyes indicative of heavy crying.

"Of course," she replied indicating the chairs. "I am sorry my husband is not home."

"Oh," Holmes appeared dismayed. "Do you know when he will return? I wished to speak with both of you."

"I do not," she answered. "To be honest, I have not seen Rufus since I heard the terrible news."

"His father told us he came straight here after he heard the news," Watson said. "He wanted you to hear it from him, I expect."

She looked at him for a moment and then burst into tears.

"My dear lady, whatever is the matter?" Watson asked pulling out his handkerchief and rushing to her side.

They waited, as she was quite unable to say anything for a moment. When she finally calmed, Holmes spoke.

"Your husband did not return like he told his father," Holmes stated. She shook her head again. "Did he know his brother was the father of your child?"

She looked up at him suddenly, her eyes wide with unfathomable terror. Watson looked over at Holmes surprised.

"How dare you make such an accusation?" She cried.

"Come now, Lady Rufus," Holmes replied unfazed. "We are not here to judge you and we have no reason to wish your secret known."

"How could you possibly..." She breathed.

"The little boy I saw peeking out of the room as we walked in is no more than three years old. Your husband is a much older man, ten years I'd say. From what your father-in-law told us, Robert came back at a time after you and your husband developed an understanding.

"Robert and Rufus fell out for some reason and Robert did not attend your wedding. Then he came back less than five years later. Your son is three. The math is not hard. When I examined the body of your brother-in-law, I noticed he had a very particular shade of green eyes," Watson knew better than to look over at Holmes. He had never examined Robert Forester's body; they were scheduled to meet with the coroner later that day. "Neither yourself, nor your husband," Holmes indicated the portrait. "Has that particular shade. The boy I saw has the same color eyes as your brother-in-law. Since eyes are hereditary to either the father or the mother, with the dominate color winning, it is easy to deduce the man lying dead in the morgue is your lover and father of your child. The question you are asking yourself now is, could your husband have known and could he have murdered his brother?"

"Rufus would never have done that!" She stood.

Holmes looked up at her again unfazed by her outburst.

"Madam, it's true the motives of women are sometimes a mystery to me, but I can assure you the motives of men seldom escape me," Holmes said. "It would be best if you tell me all."

Lady Rufus stared at him for a long moment. Swallowing hard, she finally nodded.

"Very well, Mr. Holmes, I will," she sank back onto the couch.

"Start at the beginning," Holmes instructed.

"My husband; Rufus and I met during my first season," she replied. "My father is Lord Paynetree and I am fortunate to say I had many suitors, though most of them seemed merely interested in my dowry. Then I met Rufus. His maturity I found refreshing. He was not interested in my money since he had plenty of his own. When we first met, I was taken in by his handsome features and kind smile. We were soon courting and engaged within the year. It was at our engagement party I met Robert. He was so young and full of life and interesting travels. He had just returned from Switzerland for a time. We began to see more and more of each other. Whenever Rufus was engaged with matters of state, he would send his brother to be my escort for the evening. I found myself falling in love with him. He was so unlike anyone I had ever met and it put me in a most awkward and difficult situation."

"Your engagement to Lord Rufus had already been announced and there was no way you could break that bond without somewhat of a scandal," Watson summarized.

"Precisely, Dr. Watson," she replied. "It is scandalous to admit it, but Robert and I had been meeting secretly on Hampstead Heath. It was a week before my wedding and he begged me to run away with him. I told him I could not do that to his brother. He told me he would not sit idly by and watch me marry Rufus, he could not. He told me he loved me more than Rufus ever could, but I knew my position and most of all Rufus's name. I could not allow scandal to touch him. I did care for my fiancé, but when I told Robert no for the final time, he looked broken. He warned me, my husband had a terrible temper I had never seen before. I did not believe him and to this day Rufus has never laid a hand on me in anger. Robert and my husband had a horrible row later that day and Robert left. He did not return until four years later. After a time, my husband and I gave up hope of having children. We both seemed to resign ourselves to the fate we would be barren. Then Robert returned. I will not bore you with the details, Mr. Holmes."

"Needless to say, when you two met again the feelings reignited," Holmes said.

"They never went out," she answered. "I had never been unfaithful to my husband, but it was a cosmic pull between Robert and me. Neither of us could resist, and then our son was born."

"Did your husband know?" Watson asked.

"Yes," she answered. "We told him when it was clear Howard was Robert's. Rufus was not at all what we expected. He was kind, forgiving and even thanked his brother for carrying on the family name but since he would not allow his son to be a bastard, he took Howard as his own and encouraged Robert and I to... love each other. He said he knew my heart was never fully his. He has been nothing but kind."

"Lady Rufus," Holmes started. "I must ask you, where

was your husband the night Sir Robert was murdered?"

"He left his room around two in the morning," she said.

"And where was Sir Robert?" Holmes asked. Immediately, Lady Rufus blushed and looked down. "I would not ask if it were not vital that I know the truth."

"He was with me," she finally replied. "In my room. He heard Rufus's door open and close. Robert went to the door and opened it just a crack. Seeing Rufus walk down the stairs, Robert said he did not like the look on his face and decided to follow him, claiming he had been acting strangely around him. I begged him not to, but he wouldn't listen to me," silent tears ran down her cheeks.

"Was that the last you saw your husband?" Holmes asked. She nodded. "Had you noticed him behaving strangely. You said Sir Robert had, and did not like the look on his face. Did he often leave the house at two in the morning?"

"I am sure you will forgive me, Mr. Holmes when I say I do not know. We had not shared the same room for a very long time," she explained.

"I see," Holmes said. "You have not told me everything, Lady Forester. The marks on your wrist? You said Rufus has never raised a hand to you in anger."

"They are nothing," she answered. "I know what it looks like, Mr. Holmes. My husband may be many things, but he has never been a brute. He has never hit me nor grabbed me. These marks were from my son's playroom. I fell over a misplaced toy in his room and twisted my wrist. My maid can attest to it. She even made a remark about how it might look to the rest of the world. You are free to look at it, Dr. Watson. You will see it is only a sprain. Believe me, Mr. Holmes; if my husband did this to me and with what you are saying about Robert's death, I would not hold it back from you. But what makes this all horrible is that my husband has been nothing but kind, a gentleman, a good husband and father. It is all my own doing. I should never have allowed myself to be so weak to betray my husband."

"Not at all, my dear lady," Watson said.

"Tell me, Lady Rufus, has your husband ever been to China?" Holmes asked without a second remark regarding the bruising on her wrist.

"China?" She asked. "No, why?"

"Are you quite sure? Perhaps before you were married?" Holmes asked.

"Yes, he had never ventured past Ireland to the West and France to the East, he is not a traveler," she said.

"Do you remember him ever mentioning a Professor Moriarty?" Holmes asked.

"Moriarty?"

"Yes, a Professor James Moriarty..."

"No, but surely the man is dead," she answered. "I am a follower of your works, Dr. Watson, and I recall the case where you were in Reichenbach."

Holmes said nothing in response to that. "What about Moreau?"

Watson recognized the name in the papers Marguerite used as her maiden name.

"Moreau," she repeated. "Yes, now you mention it, I do recall him mentioning that name, but I cannot remember in what setting, or why."

"Thank you, Lady Rufus, you have been most helpful. Come, Watson. Good day, my lady," Holmes stood and headed for the door.

"Mr. Holmes," she called to him. He stopped and turned to her. "You think Rufus killed Robert, don't you?"

"It is a possibility," he answered.

"I know you are a man of discretion, Mr. Holmes. I must beg you to keep what I told you to yourself."

"I believe I can swear to it, ma'am," Holmes replied.

"Rufus is a good man. I am only so sorry my lack of restraint has caused him so much pain," she said. "But when the heart knows what it wants, there is little we can do."

"Love is a mystery even I cannot solve, Lady Rufus," Holmes said. "Good day."

Chapter Thirty-Four

"All right, Holmes," Watson said once they were outside. "Who is Moreau?" Holmes said nothing. "Holmes," he called again.

"I heard you the first time, Watson. I was thinking. Moreau is the name of Marguerite's mother. It is a name close enough to Moriarty, he would use it himself on occasion."

"As an alias?" Watson asked.

"One of them," Holmes answered hailing a cab.

"Where to now?"

"Back to Soho. I want to see who may have heard or saw something that night."

Holmes sent a note to the Diogenes Club and to Baker Street telling Edmond and Percy to meet him at a Soho tavern. Percy, who was visiting his mother, sister and Cedric at Baker Street when his father's note came, was the first of his two sons to arrive.

Watson told Percy what they had discovered while speaking to Lady Rufus and watched his reaction to the information. Percy simply nodded slowly. Watson had seen that reaction so many times from Holmes, it made him roll his eyes. His main concern was how Percy reacted to the possibility of infidelity. Fortunately, he passed the test, he would be a faithful husband to Alexandra, if it came to that.

Holmes mentioned Edmond should be on his way and they should go ahead and take a seat. Before they ordered, Holmes asked the landlord about Rufus and Robert.

"Oh aye," the landlord answered. "I remember them. Two gen'lemen matchin' your description were in the other night. The first one; the one with the brown eyes, met another man over at that table," he indicated a table near the back of the pub. "The other with those peculiar green eyes you mentioned, came over and sat down pretty much where you are seated yourself, young man," he looked at Percy. "I would never have noticed his eyes, you see, Sir, but I remember me sister has the same shade back in Ireland. He also looked like he was trying not to be seen. He asked me if I knew the man with the other one who had just sat down."

"And did you?" Holmes asked.

"Well, yes, sir," he replied, uncomfortably. "It was Jameson, me sister's boy. He came over from Belfast a year ago. Ship hand, ya see, sir."

Holmes felt the suddenly charged air around Percy. Turning slightly, Holmes locked eyes with his son. Percy's nod was almost imperceptible. Homes did not respond, he merely turned back to the landlord.

"Could you describe your nephew?" he asked.

"Now, I don't want him to get into any trouble, his mother would tan my hide if I was the cause of any discomfort," he answered.

"No, no, not at all," Holmes replied in a placating voice Watson knew well. "We merely wanted to eliminate him from our inquiries. You see the man we are looking for is like your nephew," Holmes replied.

"Well, if he's not in any trouble," he started.

"Not at all," Holmes answered.

"He's twenty-two, sandy haired, a bit less than average height, rather slender," the landlord described.

"Any distinguishing marks?" Holmes asked.

"He has a large hook shaped scar on his right hand," he said. "Got it while hauling in the day's catch in Belfast three years ago. Nearly took his right thumb off."

"I see, well, it is clear the man we seek is not your nephew," Holmes lied. "Thank you all the same. We'll take three pints of your best bitter please," Holmes ordered. "And won't you have one with us?" Holmes asked producing another coin and handing it to him.

"Oh, thank you kindly, sir," he turned and filled the glasses. With the landlord's back to them, Holmes side glanced at Percy, who nodded. That was the description of the other man he and Edmond met at Moriarty's house.

"So, Lord Rufus who we now know as Murray met Jameson here the night of Sir Robert's death," Percy said as they all sat together at a back table.

"It would appear so," Holmes replied looking towards the door as Edmond walked in. Seeing his father, Edmond walked over to them and sat down beside his brother.

"Care for anything Ed?" Holmes asked.

"No, thank you, dad," Edmond replied. "Forgive me for being a little late, Uncle and I were just returning from Parliament."

"Any news on that side?" Holmes asked seeing the jade ring on his son's right middle finger.

"Some," he answered. "It looks like negotiations will be commencing. We'll talk later. But what have you found out? You said you have discovered the identity of Murray?"

"Lord Rufus Forester, Sir Robert's brother," Holmes said. Holmes briefly explained what they had discovered from Lady Rufus.

"Brother killed brother?" Edmond asked, his eyes drifting to Percy beside him. Percy nudged him teasingly and comfortingly.

"Well, yes, but Sir Robert did father a child with his brother's wife," Percy said.

"That would change any relationship," Edmond agreed.

"No matter if he claimed to be all right with the situation. You are convinced Rufus killed his brother, then? But what about the others?"

"I mentioned to Watson before; where's the best place to conceal a jewel?" Holmes said.

"In the midst of other jewels," Edmond replied.

"And the best place to hide a murder?" Holmes prompted.

"Amidst other murders," Percy answered leaning back.

"This murder has been carefully planned," Holmes went on. "Probably since he discovered Robert was the father of his child. It also helped Moriarty's plan to fund both sides of the war. This is his oldest trick. He has done this with every war we have had. He fueled the hatred of the British people by creating a serial killer and they filled in what they wanted. He has always been a master at doing that. But he also used Murray's hatred for his brother as a means to an end. Murray gets what he wants and Moriarty uses him for his own plot. All Moriarty wanted was to keep his revenue stream, namely funding the war, in full force.

"The fact I introduced you all now was just another way for him to make sure I would know it was him. Spooner's murder and the document was a smoke screen. It was all to fuel England's hatred. They did not need the documents they stole. Moriarty probably has men who helped write it. Cedric's brother's death was a personal attack against us. He chose the day Rebecca was to be presented deliberately."

"I left Cedric with Mother and Rebecca," Percy revealed. "He had not left them as you asked."

"That is welcome news," Holmes said. "But irrelevant to my explanation," Watson chortled. "As I was saying, Moriarty's main goal was to make me realize no matter what I do, his curse will remain unbroken. He will always be there."

"Not when I am finished with him," Edmond muttered.

Eyes turned to him but he merely reached over and grabbed Percy's pint and took a drink. Percy chuckled and waved to the barman ordering another.

"Holmes, you were going to explain the meanings behind the carvings in the men's foreheads," Watson said.

"You remember, Watson, when I told you about some of my earliest cases after Marguerite and I were married? I know you boys recall," he said to his sons. They nodded. All fell silent as the landlord came over and handed Percy another pint. Once he left, Holmes continued. "There was a serial killer that left a calling card. I told you this story before we met the Earl of Springfield," Watson nodded as he finally remembered. "He left the initials JM carved into the men's foreheads. It's his *modus operandi*, he always carves something. I first started my theory when I saw Spooner, the first victim nearly three months back with the YinYang engraved into his forehead. As much as I saw the similarity in the two cases, I had no evidence. I have been building a case around him, with solid evidence now."

"Perhaps it would be best if we did not have evidence," Edmond started.

"What do you mean?" Holmes asked.

"Perhaps we should finish what you started at Reichenbach Falls. Perhaps the only way to deal with a man like Moriarty is to cut off the head."

"Oh, very French, Edmond," Percy teased.

"I am being serious," Edmond replied.

"I know you are, son," Holmes said. "But no, we do not work that way. Moriarty must face trial for all the crimes he has committed."

"Forgive me for arguing with you, Dad," Edmond answered. "But what about all the others you have let escape justice or have allowed to leave because you felt it was the right thing to do. Why them and not him? I know you have thought this through but, sir there is more at stake now. Mother would be looked upon as an enemy, Percy and I would be mistrusted wherever we go and looked upon as the grandsons of Professor Moriarty. Rebecca would not be able to handle the strain of being ostracized in such a new place."

"I have thought this through, Edmond," Holmes' voice was firm.

"But, Father," Edmond started.

"One thing, Edmond," Watson interrupted him before he could continue. He saw the fire in Holmes' eyes and knew it could only lead to trouble. "Who was it you saw watching you at Mycroft's lodgings?"

Edmond must have seen it too because he broke eye contact with his father and looked over at Watson.

"The one I went after?" He clarified. Watson nodded. "That was Lord Rufus. I remember his facial hair was very distinctive with the V shaped goatee," Edmond explained.

"So this whole thing, six men dead because he was trying to get our attention?" Percy asked.

"Something like that," Holmes answered. "That, and also to cause increased hatred of the Chinese people by the British. That way the war would be sure to continue and keep Moriarty's pockets lined."

"Ambassador Geming, the Chinese leader told me there have been three murders of his countrymen since the Boxer Murders began," Edmond said. "Quite an ingenious plan, turning one country against the other and blaming that country when they had nothing to do with it. But we are at war with them already so that insures the war will continue. Then, watching the pieces fall into place and stepping in at exactly the right moment, and offering a desperate country the only possible option, all while funding the other side of the war as well."

"Worthy of your grandfather," Holmes said.

At that moment, the pub door opened and Jameson sauntered in. Percy and Edmond, their back to the door saw their father's reaction and slowly turned in their seats. Jameson smiled at his uncle, the pub keeper and he mentioned something to him, motioning to Holmes. Taking his pint of Guinness, Jameson walked over to the table. Edmond started to stand but Holmes raised a hand stopping him.

"Mr. Holmes," Jameson started his Northern Irish accent coloring his speech. "It's good to meet you."

"You have the advantage of me," Holmes replied.

"Oh, come now, I'm sure you know who I am. I know your sons do. The professor has spoken highly of you," he said. "It's good to see you both again."

"I wish I could say the same, Jameson," Percy said.

"Oh, the professor asked me to give you this if I were to

meet you," Jameson reached into his coat. Edmond stood quickly prepared to defend his family if it was something threatening. "Easy, it's merely a letter. Here, Holmes," he handed it to him. "A very good afternoon to you gentlemen," he gulped down his beer and left the pub.

When he was gone, Percy, Watson, and Edmond turned to Holmes.

"What does it say?" Percy asked.

Holmes opened it and read it in silence. His face went ashen. His fingers clenched around the paper and shook violently. His breathing increased. His features reflected rage and abhorrence. He stood so fast, he knocked the chair out from under him and it went flying toward the wall. Tossing the note over his shoulder, he ran out of the pub and disappeared.

The three of them watched Holmes rush out the door, a sick feeling coming over each of them. As Watson took the note, they soon understood why. Watson read it aloud.

"'Back where it all began'," he said. "'Marguerite and Rebecca will enjoy our time together. You know what I said I would do if you went back to her. I am looking forward to getting to know my granddaughter and I know my men are too. You know where we are. Your move, Holmes. Take your time. I will be happy to introduce them both to my men,'" Watson swallowed the bile that rose in his throat.

Percy and Edmond went stock still as they listened.

"Oh god," Percy breathed. "I'll kill him."

"Stand in line," Edmond growled as they both got up and ran after their father.

Chapter Thirty-Five

"Marguerite!" Holmes yelled frantically as he burst into the flat at 221B Baker Street. "Rebecca! Answer me!" He raced up the stairs calling their names again. When he yanked open the door to the study, his eyes scanned the room, it lay in shambles. His eyes lighted upon Cedric's unconscious form lying on the rug near the fireplace. Rushing over to him, Holmes got him up and leaned him against the arm chair. Loosening Cedric's collar button, Holmes grabbed some brandy, and poured a little into his mouth. Slowly, Cedric came around.

"Rebecca," Cedric breathed, his eyes still closed.

"Cedric, can you hear me?" Holmes called to him.

"Rebecca," Cedric breathed again. Finally, he came to with a start. "Rebecca!"

"Easy," Holmes placed a hand on Cedric's chest holding him down. Cedric turned his unfocused eyes up to Holmes.

"Where is she?" Cedric demanded.

"What do you remember? Tell me," Holmes ordered.

"I was here. Mrs. Holmes and Rebecca offered me some

tea. Percy joined us then left when he received your note. About ten minutes later, there was a noise outside and two men came into the room. One of them grabbed Rebecca, I tried to fight them but the other one hit me over the head. Everything went foggy. I remember hearing Mrs. Holmes fighting them, but they placed something over her mouth and she fainted. Rebecca screamed but last I saw, they covered her mouth too. I couldn't do anything. I don't remember anything else."

"Did you hear anything?" Holmes asked.

Cedric shook his head. "My ears were ringing." Then realization came over him. "Where are they, Mr. Holmes? Where are they?"

Holmes heard Watson, Percy and Edmond on the stair. He yelled for Watson, who ran faster than the others. Once Watson got to Cedric, Holmes left him and went to his sons.

"Come with me, we have work to do," he said dangerously calm. "Watson, when you're done here, take the next train to Yorkshire. Then follow the directions back to Moriarty's estate. You can find your way back there?"

"Yes, of course," Watson answered, as he examined Cedric.

"Mr. Holmes, I'm so sorry. I should have protected them," Cedric lamented. "Please, let me come with you. I must be there. I... I, Rebecca means to world to me."

"I know," Holmes replied. "When Watson says it's all right you can join him. Until then, Percy, Edmond, come with me."

Marguerite slowly woke, unaware of her surroundings. All she could remember was seeing Rebecca being grabbed by one of the two men who burst into their home and Cedric trying to protect them but he was hit. She remembered fighting, but it was blurry.

As she woke, she felt the jockeying of a carriage. Opening her eyes with a start, she looked around the area. Rebecca was beside her, still unconscious. Marguerite breathed a quick sigh of relief, and then looked around her. No one else was in the carriage. The windows were covered with a black substance, paint probably, and she could not see out. She tried the door, it was locked or something prevented it from opening. Easing her daughter towards her, she gently tried to wake her up.

"Rebecca?" She called.

Rebecca groaned and shifted slightly.

"Rebecca, wake up, *ma cherie*," Marguerite said.

Finally, Rebecca opened her eyes. Then suddenly, as if she remembered what happened, she looked around panicked.

"Where are we?" She cried.

"Shh, it's all right, *mon coeur*," Marguerite said. "Listen to me, everything is all right."

"Where's Cedric?" She begged.

"I do not know," Marguerite answered.

"What's going on, Mama? What's going to happen?" Rebecca questioned.

"Rebecca, look at me," Marguerite held her daughter's face in her hands. "I do not know what is happening or why. But I will tell you what *will* happen. Your father and brothers will be coming after us and god help whoever it is that took us. I need you to be strong, my love. Know that I am here and no matter what happens, you will survive."

Rebecca took a deep breath, raised her head high and nodded once.

"That's my girl," Marguerite gently rubbed her thumb over Rebecca's cheeks wiping away her tears.

The carriage came to a stop and they both heard the crunch of gravel beneath someone's feet as they walked around the carriage. Rebecca held onto her mother's hand as the door opened. A man with a V shaped goatee and black hair stood in front of them.

"Get out," he ordered.

"Who are you? What do you want with us?" Marguerite demanded not moving to get out of the carriage.

"Get out," the man ordered again.

"Not until you tell me who you are and what we are doing here," she countered.

Exasperated, he reached in and grabbed Marguerite's wrist. Pulling her out of the carriage, he threw her down to the gravel. Crying out, she landed on her wrist and shooting pain went up her arm as she felt a crack.

"Mama!" Rebecca screamed from the carriage.

Marguerite looked back up at the man who had grabbed her, her face pale from the pain but anger bubbled to the surface.

"I told you to get out," he shrugged.

"My husband is going to enjoy killing you, but until then," she replied. "There's something my son taught me to do," she swept her leg from behind him, knocking him to the ground. He fell onto his back with a thud. He got up just as fast as he fell, and seized her by her hair, cursing as he went. Marguerite twisted and with her good hand, jabbed him in the groin causing him to double over. He raised his hand to her and was about to hit her when someone from behind them spoke.

"Murray," the voice called. The man stopped and looked towards the voice. "Let her go."

"Sir, she—" he started.

"I know," the voice giggled. "I saw the whole thing. Release her."

Murray relinquished his grip on Marguerite's hair. She turned to face the man who had stopped Murray, but when she saw his face, her heart plummeted to her feet and she broke into a cold sweat.

"Hello, my dear," Moriarty grinned at her. "Welcome home."

"Mama," Rebecca's voice came from behind her. Having just gotten out of the carriage, Rebecca clutched at her mother's left arm. "Who is it?"

Marguerite turned to her daughter ignoring the scream of pain from her wrist as she clutched her daughter's hands.

"He is your grandfather, Becca," she explained. "Do not trust him. Fight with every fiber of your being, do you understand me?"

"*That* is Moriarty?" Rebecca asked, her voice small.

"Yes," Margot replied.

Rebecca eyed him. "I thought he'd be much taller."

Marguerite had to cover her laugh but cupped her face. "I had a feeling it was him, but I hoped I was wrong. Be strong, your father and brothers will be here soon."

"Come in, won't you?" Moriarty continued.

Marguerite finally looked around. She knew the place at once; the ancestral estate where she had spent three years of her life, the happiest and most horrible moments of her existence.

Both women took each other's hands, walked up the steps and followed him into the ancient building.

A flood of memories overwhelmed Marguerite and she remembered the first time they had danced as she walked into the ballroom...

"Miss Moriarty," Sherlock walked over to her. Marguerite turned to him and smiled.

"Mr. Holmes," she greeted him with a small curtsey.

"Might I have this dance?" He asked.

"With pleasure," she replied slipping her fingers into his hand.

...when she caught Sherlock and Mycroft breaking into the secret room in the wall with the mechanism inside the fireplace...

"Don't you understand?" Holmes said. "He's a criminal!"

"He's my father. How could you betray him like this?" She demanded.

"Marguerite, listen to me," he started.

"Sherlock, we have to go," Mycroft's voice came from the shadows.

"I can't, Mycroft," he said.

"You must, come on, come with me," Mycroft replied.

"If you ever loved me," Holmes said to her. "Do not raise the alarm."

...and lastly the final night when Moriarty shot him after Holmes begged her to come away with him and they shared their first passionate kiss.

"Margot, you have to come with me, please you have to," Holmes begged.

"I cannot," she replied. "He's my father."

"I love you, you know that. I want to be with you. I want to marry you. Please come with me, Margot. I cannot live without you," she had never seen him cry but a single tear slid down his cheek as he spoke. She wiped it gently away.

"If you love me, then you know me, and you know I could never do what you ask," she replied. "I love you, Sherlock, more than anything, but I cannot go with you, not like this."

"He will kill you," Holmes' voice was staccato. She breathed deeply.

"That is something I will have to deal with on my own," she said.

"On your own?" Holmes demanded. "Woman, don't you understand, without you I am nothing? I am a machine. When I am with you, I see myself through your eyes. I start to see my potential. I do not want to go back to the way I was before I met you, Margot. I want to be the man you see me as. A man who wants to love you the way you deserve to be loved." She began to cry. "Please, come with me," he begged again.

She felt his hands on her face, then his lips on hers in their first truly passionate kiss.

Marguerite still felt the tingle of his kiss on her lips that day as she stepped into the once stunning ballroom.

Chapter Thirty-Six

"Mama?" Rebecca's voice brought Marguerite back to the present. They were standing in the ballroom, its grandeur, an age gone by. For a moment, she saw it as it once was, the music playing from the gallery, friends dancing under the flickering lights of the chandelier, her portrait, painted for her on her seventeenth birthday hanging above the fireplace. Her eyes drifted towards it, but the only thing she saw was an outline of dust where the frame had been. She swallowed away the tears that threatened.

"Welcome home, my dears," Moriarty sneered as he stood in front of them. "So sorry for the state of everything, I had to leave rather quickly twenty-six years ago, but I'm sure you recall that evening, do you not, Marguerite?"

The sound of her name on his lips sent shivers down her spine. Moriarty once cared deeply for her and she felt so loved by him but now, the look on his face and the tone of his voice told her he would rather kill her. For a moment Marguerite heard the echo of the gunshot from all those years ago and in her mind's eye saw Holmes fall in front of her when the bullet hit his chest. The scar was one she traced often, remembering how he stepped in front of her, certain it was meant for her.

"What do you want with us?" She asked.

"Holmes," he answered simply. "He knows what I would do if he ever saw you again and from the looks of it, he saw a great deal of you several times," he looked at Rebecca. "I roused his interest with these Boxer murders, now I want him. I've always thought we would make a good team. But you stand in the way of that, you have always stood in the way of that."

"So you are going to kill me?" Marguerite asked.

"Hmm, not yet," Moriarty answered. "He needs to be here. He needs to see it."

"Moriarty!" Holmes voice boomed through the house.

"Papa!" Rebecca screeched.

Holmes ran into the ball room the next second. Rebecca rush towards him. He hugged her tightly for a moment.

"Are you all right?" He demanded pulling back from his daughter and looking at her. His hands framed her face. She nodded. He wiped her tears away and held her close to him again.

His eyes raced to his wife. She told him all he needed to know in that one look. He pushed Rebecca behind him and felt her arms wrap around his waist. She held on to him as she had when she was a little girl, her head buried between his shoulder blades.

"I'm here now, Moriarty," Holmes said. "Let them go."

"You can have *one* of them. I'm sure my grandsons are out there, so," he pulled out a gun and aimed it at Marguerite's head while Murray grabbed her arms preventing her from defending herself. Jameson came up behind Holmes and grabbed Rebecca. She screamed as she was torn away from her father. Holmes turned and saw Jameson had a knife to her throat, tears rained down her cheeks.

"Wait," Holmes roared. He stepped forward closer to the middle between the two most important women in his life. Raising his hands, one toward Rebecca and the other toward Moriarty, "Just wait," he said.

"Ooh, this is more enjoyable than I imagined it would

be," Moriarty jeered. "Choose who you will watch die. The other is free to go."

Holmes looked at Marguerite. She nodded at him.

"Let Rebecca go," Holmes ordered.

"Exactly what I thought, so very predictable," Moriarty motioned Jameson to let her go.

"Papa!" Rebecca screamed.

"Go, Becca!" Holmes ordered. "Your brothers are outside."

"No!" She cried seeing the look between her parents; Holmes never dropped Marguerite's eyes.

"I said go!" Holmes commanded.

Rebecca looked passed him to her mother. Marguerite broke contact with her husband for a moment to look at her daughter.

"*Vas-y*," Marguerite ordered her daughter to go. Rebecca shook with unshed tears but ran out of the room to her brothers outside. Marguerite looked back at Holmes and held his gaze. Moriarty watched them both, his ultimate goal, to make Sherlock suffer, was finally within his grasp.

"Jameson, do the honors," Moriarty said. Holmes felt the prod of a knife in his lower back, coaxing him forward. There was a chair near to Moriarty facing the door and Jameson pressed Holmes' shoulder down forcing him to sit in the chair. Holmes allowed Jameson to tie both of his wrists to the arms of the chair and both of his ankles to the legs.

Moriarty motioned Marguerite over. He forced her to face her husband. Murray kicked the back of her knees to make her kneel and she fell hard on the marble floor. Closing her eyes at the pain that rushed through her, she took a deep breath but did not cry out. Holmes saw how she held her right wrist close to her body. She moved her sleeve slightly and he saw the bruising and swelling that had already begun. Holmes gripped the arms of the chairs so tightly his arms shook. Moriarty walked up behind Marguerite and stood with his gun at the back of her head.

"No," Holmes breathed, his worst nightmare coming true and he was powerless. Marguerite closed her eyes, praying silently.

"It's very simple, Holmes, I have always known your worth ever since I was your tutor at University. I always thought you and I would make an unstoppable team and when I found out who your father was, I knew there was just enough criminal in you to be useful. But because you fell in love with this woman, I lost a valuable ally. You always, doggedly went after me to no success. Even your greatest success, Reichenbach Falls, was hampered by a convenient tree branch that I could hold on to. I did not come out completely unscathed as you see," he motioned to the scar on his face. "But still, you were bested yet again. So, you have two choices. Stop coming after me and tell the world you are a failure, or watch the woman you love die with a bullet through her brain. I told you what I would do if you went back to her. Well, it just took me longer than I expected...

"You know, we are not unalike, you and I. We both think we are better than everyone else and truth be told, we are rather, but we're more like the YinYang, Light and Dark. We bring balance to this rundown world of ours. We are the life force but imagine how much more powerful we could have been together. It's such a pity you followed your heart instead of your head. Odd, isn't that what you always warn Watson about?

"I'm tired of this game we're playing. You have been a thorn in my side for far too long. I told you in this very room, I would be your curse. Well, I never realized until it was too late, that you are my curse. I want to live out the rest of my days with the knowledge that I won, I beat you," he laughed. "It's rather a nice feeling, I must say. So, the choice is yours. What's it going to be?"

Holmes stared up at him. Finally, he began speaking in a mocking tone but as he continued, his voice became more and more heated.

"You think you're a god, don't you?" Holmes started. "Messing with the lives of others, making them do what you want, torturing those around you whether they deserve it or not, taking the lives that might have been by using and changing the people involved, forcing them to bend to your will. You think just because others have fallen into your trap, everyone will. Well... I'm not everyone and I am tired of living my life hiding, out of fear of you and what you're capable of. I am not your puppet and my life and the lives of those I love are not in your hands. You can do whatever you want to me, but know this, no matter what you do, no matter what you take from me, I will never be like you. I will never surrender to you.

"So go ahead, take it! Take what you want! I know those I love will always be mine and nothing you do will ever change that! You are just an old, tired, bitter, angry man with nothing to live for anymore. So you take and take and take and take from others trying to make them as miserable as you are. Well, I have news for you, nothing you do, can ever make me like you. Take my family, take my life, but you will never break my spirit because I have had the love of the most incredible woman in the universe. She has stood by me no matter what and if you take her from me you will live with the knowledge that you have not succeeded in bringing me down, you have only signed your own death warrant because I will not stop until you are dead by my hand. So, if you want to live out your days looking over your shoulder, then go ahead, pull that trigger. Take the last angel from this earth. Complete your mission, but in penance you will have the mind of a mad man tracking you down until your blood runs through his fingers. Today, I swear, if you take her life, you will die with my name on your lips and I will be the last thing you see on this earth until Hell itself welcomes you with open arms."

Moriarty stared at him for a long moment, and then he began to laugh.

"Say goodbye, Sherlock Holmes," he said. Holmes broke the arms of the chair and dived for his wife.

"Now, Edmond!" He shouted.

Moriarty turned to see what was going on. Holmes covered Marguerite's body with his own as a loud gunshot shattered the silence followed by two others a little quieter. Burying his head into Marguerite's neck as he heard glass shatter, Holmes told her to stay still. After everything went quiet, Holmes looked back to see his son shouldering a rifle. Moriarty, Murray and Jameson lay around the room where Edmond had shot them.

"Cut it a bit close, didn't you, Ed?" Holmes breathed.

"It's what I do," Edmond replied just before he collapsed onto the floor in a heap.

"Edmond!" Holmes exclaimed, racing to his son. "Watson!" He shouted as he ripped his son's jacket and vest open. Marguerite reached Edmond at the same time as Holmes did and gently cradled her son's head in her lap. She soothed his face as Holmes frantically searched for the wound. It didn't take him long. The amount of blood their only clue to a bullet wound in Edmond's side. Out of reflex, Holmes tore off his own jacket and applied pressure to the wound. Edmond flinched and reared up as pain assaulted his every sense.

"Move, Holmes!" Watson commanded. Holmes did, and Watson began examining the wound. "The bullet is still in there. We have to get him to the hospital."

"I want you to do it," Holmes replied.

"I may have been a field surgeon, Holmes but I am a general practitioner now. I have not dealt with gun shots in years," Watson retorted.

"I don't trust anyone else!" Holmes yelled.

Watson looked at his friend's eyes. He had never seen Holmes panic, but he was frightened now. Watson finally nodded.

"He'll bleed out if we don't hurry," Watson said.

"Edmond, stay with me, son," Holmes pleaded as he lifted him in his arms and carried him and followed Watson to another room.

Chapter
Thirty-Seven

The sound of his father's panic-stricken voice slowly slipped away and Edmond's eyes closed.

He felt strange, almost as if he was weightless. The warm morning sun on his face made him open his eyes. The French countryside stretched before him. He was home. His eyes scanned the old house and he took off running. Suddenly the landscape changed, it became grey and misty. Looking around he didn't know where he was, all he knew was that he was caught in a maze garden.

"Edmond," he heard faintly around him. Each member of his family called out to him. He took off running toward the voices. He didn't want to be alone. Stopping for a second, he looked up seeing a part of the fog clear. His uncle's estate loomed before him. In one window, he saw Mycroft gazing out across the garden. Edmond waved up to him and shouted his name, but Mycroft did not respond. Edmond was alone again as Mycroft turned away. He felt an emptiness grow inside him. He always wanted an escape but not like this. Running again trying to find a way out of this maze, he did not know if there was an end. Finally, he could run no longer, his lungs burned, and his legs felt like jelly. A terrible sickening feeling overcame him, and he let the most horrid, guttural scream escape him as he collapsed to his knees. For the first time in his life, he wept. He felt so alone. So cold. So silent. He didn't know how long he sat there but, faintly, through the soundless silence he heard a voice.

"Edmond," the voice whispered. "Edmond."

He looked up but couldn't see anything. The voice had a familiar sound to it.

"Uncle?" he whispered.

"Edmond, where are you?" the voice whispered again.

"I'm here, sir, I'm here," he called. He tried to stand but his legs wouldn't let him. His side hurt and he tried to take deep breaths to help with the lack of air. It did no good. The voice didn't answer him. Worried he had been lost yet again, he called out once more "Uncle?"

He hunched back on his heels and lowered his head when there was no answer. It seemed like ages. He didn't cry. He knew where he was. He knew he was dead.

Then suddenly like a deafening yell out of the silence, the voice whispered again.

"Edmond," this time it was so very close to him and a hand gently touched his hair. He looked up.

"Edmond," his father's voice surprised him.

"Dad?" He breathed.

"What are you doing here?" Holmes whispered. Edmond couldn't think of an answer. "It's time to come home, son. Come with me." Holmes extended a hand to his son and as Edmond reached for it, Holmes took it in a firm grasp.

"I'm too weak to get up," Edmond said.

"No, you're not," Holmes replied.

Edmond felt a shockwave flow through his father's hand, giving him the strength to stand.

Holmes kept his hand in his and walked slowly in the opposite direction. Holmes didn't speak. They walked for a couple of minutes. The fog lifted and Edmond saw the entrance to the maze. He smiled and almost took his hand out of his father's grip.

"Don't let go," Holmes' voice was firm. His hold intensified on his son's hand and they walked on further.

Walking under the foliaged archway, Edmond looked up and saw he was back in France. He felt his father's grasp release him and he ran towards the house but stopped suddenly and looked back. Holmes still stood in the archway of the maze.

"Aren't you coming?" Edmond asked.

"You're safe, that's all that matters to me," he said.

"What are you saying?" Edmond asked confused.

"I love you, Edmond. Never forget that." Holmes turned and walked back into the maze.

"Dad!" Edmond yelled and hurriedly rushed towards him, but a wind knocked him onto his back with a force that shook the ground. "Dad!" He screamed.

"Easy, easy," Watson's voice broke the silence as he held Edmond down.

Looking around the room, he saw they were in a hospital. He was alive.

"Where's my father?" He demanded.

Watson nodded his head indicating the bed beside him. Edmond looked over and saw Holmes lying unconscious, his hand lying limp over the edge of the cot as if he had held Edmond's. Edmond saw the bandage around Holmes's arm and a similar one on his arm.

"What happened?" Edmond demanded.

Chapter Thirty-Eight

Several hours earlier

"What do you need?" Holmes demanded as he laid his son's body on the table in the dining room.

"Instruments, fluids and you and Marguerite out of here," Watson said.

"Absolutely not," Holmes replied.

"You're of no help to me."

"Doctor, I'm staying."

Watson had no time to argue. Grabbing his medical bag and opening it, he pulled out the various instruments he would need. Laying out his handkerchief on another small table, he laid his instruments out. Not as sterile as he would have hoped but it would have to do. He had worked in less sterile conditions.

As he went about his work, Marguerite stood near the door and out of their way. Holmes followed Watson's instructions and was more useful than he anticipated. Edmond passed out from the pain and loss of blood shortly after Holmes had laid him on the table.

Percy, Rebecca and Cedric ran in. Rebecca screeched

when she saw the amount of blood on Holmes' shirt and Watson's hands. She fell into Cedric who held her tightly to him. Percy raced to his father.

"What can I do?" He demanded.

"Go to your mother," Holmes ordered. "Watson and I have this well in hand."

Percy nodded once and rushed to his mother, who was silent by the door, her rosary beads in her hands.

"Cedric, get her out of here!" Holmes yelled.

Cedric had to drag Rebecca out of the room, but they were eventually alone with only Marguerite and Percy standing at the doorway.

It was about fifteen minutes later when Watson finally got the bullet out but then cursed violently as blood began pouring out of the wound.

"What is it?" Holmes demanded.

"He's losing too much blood," Watson said. "I was able to get the bullet out but he's gushing right now. Give me the needle and thread over there, quickly," Holmes grabbed what Watson needed and handed it to him. Watson's concentration was absolute. Holmes held Edmond down as Watson placed the stiches. After an agonizing few minutes, Watson sealed the stiches and checked Edmond's pulse.

"Dammit," Watson cursed again.

"What now?" Holmes asked.

"He's lost too much blood. He's not responding. He may never wake if he doesn't get more. Is there a compatible donor?" Watson asked.

Holmes looked at his friend for a moment then back at his son on the table. Without hesitation, he rolled up his shirt sleeve.

"Me," he said offering his arm. "Do it, Watson."

"Father!" Percy cried.

"Quiet, Percy, you're not compatible and neither is your mother," Holmes said not looking at him. "We discovered that several years ago or have you forgotten?"

"There's no knowing how much blood he'll need, Holmes, you could—" Watson started.

"Do you think I care about that?" Holmes demanded.

"He's my son. Do it!"

Watson looked over at Marguerite who remained motionless. After a moment, Watson nodded.

"Lie down," Watson ordered. Holmes lay beside his son on the long table. Marguerite came around the other side of him and stroked her husband's hair. He looked over at her as Watson worked.

"I love you," she said.

"I know," Holmes answered.

"I'll be here when you wake up," she stated.

"You better be," he said.

She leaned down to him and fused her lips to his. Their lips moved in perfect rhythm with each other; giving and taking, gentle and fierce, passionate and sweet. Holmes grabbed the nape of her neck and his fingers tangled gently in her hair. He kissed her like a starving man. He gave no quarter, no rest, even though it was only a few seconds, it felt like hours.

Holmes broke away from the heart stopping kiss and immediately rested his forehead against his wife's. They breathed heavily and in unison but said nothing for a moment. Finally, Holmes opened his eyes and looked deeply into his wife's brown ones.

"I love you," Holmes whispered.

"You better," she breathed.

"Marguerite," Watson said. "I'm afraid I need to ask you to leave."

She nodded and stood. She held Holmes' hand until she was too far away to touch him. Percy guided her out of the room and shut the door behind him.

"No matter what happens, Watson," Holmes turned to look at his friend. "You save my son."

Watson took a deep breath but nodded and inserted the tube into the vein in Edmond's arm. Holmes took Edmond's hand and closed his eyes as he felt the painful prick of the needle, the feeding of a tube into his arm and the blood his son needed flowing out of him and into Edmond's body.

Epilogue

Edmond sat by the window looking out to the English garden maze that had been his torment in his dream. Ever since he was a boy and he got lost in the Parisian gardens of Versailles, one of his most dreaded fears was to be caught in another and never able to find his way out.

He remembered little of his deathlike dream but as he watched the fog roll in and dusk fall, he had to suppress the irrational fear of being trapped in the maze below. Taking a deep breath, he flinched as a sharp shooting pain struck his side. The sound of his brother's piano playing accompanied by Alexandra Watson's laughter and flirtation echoed down the long halls. Holding onto that reality, he was able to separate fact from fiction. He always enjoyed his brother's playing and dearly wished he was strong enough to accompany him on his violin, but he could hardly lift a finger at the moment.

Feeling someone walk up behind him, he let them stand there looking out of the window without speaking.

"Not exactly France," the voice finally said after several long minutes of silence.

"And yet, it's strangely comforting. Almost like a second home. But it also... scares me," Edmond admitted. "Do you think he's out there somewhere?" Edmond asked after a moment looking out at the maze garden. The person behind him sighed.

"I think he is," they answered.

"And it's my fault."

"No," the voice breathed. "Not at all."

"I feel like it is," he said. "If I had just made sure, if I hadn't..."

The man walked around the wheelchair Edmond sat in and knelt before him.

"Son, Moriarty is the most devious man alive. Just because he may have worn some sort of protection under his shirt, preventing your shot from killing him, does not mean it's your fault," he said.

Edmond stared deeply into his father's eyes, his own color gray mirrored in the foggy depths.

"I'm just so very glad you are all right," Holmes said.

"I would not have been without you," Edmond answered. "Dr. Watson told me what you did for me. He told me you could have died."

"And what would I have cared if I had?" Holmes asked. "As long as my son lives... my life is worth something. You, your mother, Percy and Rebecca mean more to me than my own life. I would do it a hundred times over again as long as you survive. I never wanted my children to want for anything I was able to give, but the most important thing I can give you, is life."

"You give so much more, dad," Edmond replied. "I am honored to be your son."

Holmes gently touched his son's face. "The honor is mine, Edmond. But come now, your mother is waiting for us."

Holmes got behind his son and unlocked the wheelchair. As Holmes wheeled him away from the window, Edmond breathed deeply and closed his eyes. As he did, he heard a loud scream and recognized it as his own when he was trapped in the maze. Taking a shaky breath, Edmond quelled the fear and nausea that rose in his belly. Holmes stopped pushing the chair and looked down at him.

"Everything all right?" He asked.

"Will be," Edmond nodded.

Holmes watched him. Edmond had told him of his

dream when Holmes had awoken. The strange thing was, Holmes had experienced the exact same dream down to the last detail. That made Mycroft's estate the perfect choice for both of their convalescences. Edmond knew he had to face his demons, but Holmes didn't like what it was doing to him. Edmond would wake up screaming and not remember why, and then the next morning, he would ask Holmes to take him out into the maze garden. He would try and get out of the wheelchair and walk a little. His legs were not affected by the bullet but due to the massive loss of blood, he was still too weak to walk on his own.

Holmes knew to say nothing more and pushed his son's chair on to the dining room where Marguerite waited, hoping the worst was behind them.

Moriarty watched Edmond and Holmes at the window. His hiding place five hundred feet away on the moor, afforded him an excellent view. He observed them talking and saw how weak Edmond looked. He smirked as he thought about what he wanted to do. He would eliminate the Holmes bloodline. It would all start with him. Moving slightly, Moriarty felt the sting of the wound in his shoulder where Edmond's buck shot had gotten around his protective vest.

"You've eluded me long enough, Holmes," Moriarty said. "Let the final game commence. Checkmate in five moves... coming to play?"

FINIS

Acknowledgements

Oddly, this is the hardest part of writing a book. I never want to leave anyone out but I cannot possibly remember everyone who has had a part in this!

Firstly, I want to thank my family who have always stood by me and encouraged me throughout this whole process.

My mother, your love for Sherlock Homes has spilled over to me! Now I celebrate the next generation of Holmes'. You have always encouraged me in this novel thinking it a wonderful idea!

My dad and my editor, you meticulously went through this novel editing the grammar for me. I know... it was an arduous process especially when you began speaking in nineteenth century English! Thank you!

My wonderful friend Kate Roth! Thank you for all you have done!! The cover looks amazing and the formatting wasn't too bad! Stay awesome!

Finally to Sherlock Holmes's creator, Sir Arthur Conan Doyle. Thank you for your genius in creating a character who has transcended time! He will be forever immortal because your adoring public will never let him die! The game's afoot once again!

Some people who have read early copies of this novel asked me why did I chose to write about a fictional family. The answer is twofold. In all of Doyle's works, Sherlock Holmes painted women as the bane of his existence, a manipulative, untrustworthy, and unintelligent lot. His protestations brought to mind the famous line in Shakespeare's Hamlet: "The Lady doth protest too much." That coupled with the lines from Doyle himself in the letter to Watson at the Final Problem: "I write these few lines through the courtesy of Mr. Moriarty, who awaits my convenience for the final discussion of those questions which lie between us." Showed me that there must be something, some little known secret that Holmes, the master of disguise and secrecy did not want Watson to know. But what? Then the idea that he was keeping the most important fact about himself a secret made me think, it had something to do with Moriarty. Thus, Soundless Silence was born. There had been many different variations of this story, but this seemed the best way to introduce my discovery to the world. I hope you all enjoyed!

www.ingramcontent.com/pod-product-compliance
Lightning Source LLC
Chambersburg PA
CBHW051133020726
47501CB00005B/1485